THE COMPANION AND OTHER STORIES

MADELINE GRACE ANIANS

Edited by
LEE ANIANS-MUELLER

PLAYEDWELL
PUBLISHING

For my new family. Cathy, Jim, and Don. And to all the grandchildren, great-grandchildren, and every decedent of Madeline Anians.

INTRODUCTION

Madeline Grace McCann was my grandmother. She was born in 1904 and grew up in Ontario, Canada. Around 1927 she met and married my grandfather, James Vincent Anians who grew up in Wellington, Shropshire, England and they settled in Chicago, Illinois. I would love to relate stories about them, but unfortunately, I never met my grandparents. It wasn't until 2018 that I met anyone from the paternal side of my family. Any stories related were from my sibling's memories.

My grandfather passed away in 1969 and it appears Madeline occupied her time writing stories; it was this information that solved a riddle for me. You see, my mother's side of the family dabbled in painting and ceramics, and while I was no stranger to oil and canvas; I preferred creating images with words. From an early age, I wrote stories, beginning in grade school all the way into college. It was one of the outlets of my creative urges. I chose words over watercolor landscapes and acrylic tableaus. I was always curious as to where the storytelling inclination originated as if were carried in the DNA like eye and hair color. If it is, it was passed onto me by Madeline Grace Anians. I had a connection to a lady I never met but I wish I could have known.

She passed away in 1999 but perhaps I could meet her through her writing.

My sister gave me several of our grandmother's manuscripts; a short mystery and two historical romance-flavored tales. Two were neatly typed out with minor pencil corrections and one gave up the printed ghost halfway through and moved forward written out in long hand. What had Madeline planned to do with her writings? Did she have her sights set on becoming an author? Did she plan to submit her work to a publisher or were they for her own amusement? Some grandmothers collect commemorative plates or spoons from each state, I had one who captured her imagination on paper.

I had self-published many of my plays and a collection of short stories, so I thought, why not transcribe her prose onto the computer, format it into a book, and publish it? If it had been a dream of hers, I could make it happen. If it had not, I'll ask her forgiveness when I see her. I checked with my siblings, got their blessing, and set about the steady task of moving her words from the paper into the computer.

I remained true to her prose as she had typed it on the page. Only a few times, did I correct a word or punctuation. And yes, I felt I came to know her through her writing. She struck me as very much the romantic. She loved to describe settings, clothes, and her characters. She also loved to modify her dialogue with adverbs. You will know the tone and attitude of every character who speaks. I can imagine she was influenced by the romance literature and style of the time and a touch or two of Jane Austin. I can imagine her seeing a film or reading a book and taking inspiration to create a story of her own.

The Cavendish Pearls is very much a nod to Sherlock Holmes and is set of course in England. Once Fresh And New uses South Carolina as a backdrop and I detect some influence of Margaret Mitchell going on here. This, by the way, was the story that was written out in pen. I can not say with certainty that Madeline had completed this one for it seems to end rather abruptly, but it may have been her intention.

The Companion returns to England to tell a tale of a young girl who is hired by a wealthy family to look after the matriarch of the family. I detect an influence of Charlotte Brontë flowing in this story yet Madeline makes it her own.

I believe getting to know someone solely through their artistic work is a unique journey. It's a glimpse into their imagination and their thoughts. You learn what details are important to them, and how they convey the information which may be a hint at how they see the world and view life. Is it a complete picture of the person? No. The Madeline Grace Anians that moved through everyday life, that spoke, smiled, laughed, and cried, I can only imagine those moments from stories I am told. And perhaps we all will get to know her through these stories she wrote.

-Lee Anians-Mueller

CAVENDISH PEARLS

CAVENDISH PEARLS

I was resting comfortably in my favorite easy chair and, having solved another case a fortnight before, was by no means anxious to interrupt my leisure. The front door tinkled; and Mrs. Kyle, wiping her hands on her white starched apron, hurried down the hall to answer it.

I heard a cultured masculine voice say most insistently, "My good woman, I must speak with the Inspector at once!" My house-keeper mumbled something or other and showed a tall, distin-guished gentleman into my comfortable sanctum.

"I humbly beg your pardon if I have inconvenienced you, Inspector Lemont," the stranger began apologetically. "May I introduce myself, sir? I'm Lord Cavendish from Adderbury, needing your assistance desperately."

"Of course, your Lordship," I replied mildly. "Won't you please be seated?"

My handsome visitor seated himself opposite me. Then, searching my face with soft gray eyes said, "Inspector, let me explain my reason for coming here. Last Christmas, I happily presented my wife, Lady Pamela, with a necklace of lustrous pearls. These fine jewels were deposited each night in a safety vault in my private sitting room, the small enclosure is built snugly into the wall behind an oil painting; and I'm the only person knowing the lock combination. This morning I had occa-sion to visit my sitting room and there, to my utter amazement, I found the vault door wide open! Private papers of mine were strewn on the floor and the velvet jewel box in which the pearls were kept was empty. Being aware of your fine reputation for solving crimes, I quickly ordered my carriage and came here. Now, sir, will you help me?"

I studied the gentleman closely as he nervously straightened his ascot tie, awaiting my answer. I could see that he was a true aristocrat. I told him I would take the case, and he thanked me profusely; then getting up, I started walking back and forth in front of him.

"Now my Lord," I began, in a business-like fashion, "I shall require the names of your entire household."

"Most certainly, Inspector," Lord Cavendish replied with vigor. He paused momentarily, then went on. "Let me see; there is Giles, my valet, and Merton, the butler who, by the way, is an old family retainer. Then there is the gardener Caldwell, and Mrs. Bean, my cook and housekeeper, and of course my groom Bertie. Oh yes, there's also a new member of my staff. Lady Cavendish's French maid, Doree, who has been with us a fortnight or so."

Again, his Lordship hesitated, frowning a little. "Inspector, let me say at this point," he continued, "that I've been quite satisfied with all of them except Caldwell. I cannot abide the man's uncouth tongue and surly manner and would dismiss him promptly, only he is a proficient gardener."

I listened attentively to his remark about Caldwell, writing the name down in my notebook along with others.

"Your Lordship," I asked slowly, "did this man Caldwell present you with satisfactory references when you hired him?"

"Oh yes indeed, Inspector, the fellow came to me highly recommended by the Earl of Weymouth."

"Oh, I see." Said I, putting my notebook in my waistcoat pocket.

Lord Cavendish rose and I, with my squat, bulky frame, felt quite insignificant in the shadow of his towering height, as I stood in front of him. He impressed me deeply, and the case challenged my wits in a way not to be ignored. Looking up at him, I said respectfully.

"Your Lordship, I shall do my utmost recovering the pearls." The fine gentleman's neatly trimmed beard parted in a gleaming white smile.

"Excellent, Inspector. Then I shall expect you tomorrow at Cavendish Manor?" I nodded and accompanied him to my front door, bidding him good-day in a most friendly manner.

Early the next morning I set out for Cavendish Manor, upon my faithful mare Dolly. Mrs. Kyle, seemingly content with the prospect of my absence, was already uprooting my household for a general springtime cleaning. Being a creature of solid habits and comfort, I was quite pleased making my escape.

Riding along the dusty path away from my cottage, I decided to stop at the Tankard's Inn and ask my bright young friend Thomas Malachee to aid me on this case. I had high regard for the amiable and intelligent lad. As I guided Dolly onto the main road leading to the Inn, a soft breeze came up wafting the sweet scent of clover in from the meadow. Closing my eyes, I inhaled deeply, going into a sort of trance. But the clatter of Dolly's hooves on the pebbled road soon brought me back to the moment.

I began to think seriously about the missing pearls and, giving Dolly her head for a while, I studied the names I'd written down in my notebook. The case promised to be an interesting one.

At the Inn entrance, I dismounted nimbly and, going inside, made my way to the refreshment room where I found Thomas deep in conversation with a friend. Upon seeing me, he immediately excused himself and came forward.

"Inspector Lemont!" The Lad exclaimed, wringing my hand. "What a pleasure seeing you again." He eyed me closely. "What brings you here, Inspector? Do you plan on staying with us for a while?" His cheery face crinkled in a wide grin.

"My lad," I answered, returning his smile. "I want to speak with you. Come, let us sit down." I then led him by the arm across the room to a rear booth; and over a glass of delicious ale acquainted him with the event of Lord Cavendish's visit and the missing pearls.

"Thomas, will you assist me on this case?" I asked. He had been leaning across the table listening earnestly to all I'd said and there was an anxious gleam in his splendid blue eyes. He now sat erect and with an air of great seriousness, answered me.

"Inspector, I am at your service."

"Thank you, my lad," I replied, somewhat pleased with myself.

Thomas sat silently for a while. I could tell by his expression that he was pondering the case.

"Inspector," he said at last. "Don't you suppose the gardener is the most likely suspect?"

"Now my lad," I answered patiently, "we mustn't jump to conclusions this early in the case—we must examine it from afar fitting the pieced together one by one." I rose then, pushing back my chair. "Come, Thomas, let us be on our way."

"Right you are Inspector!" Exclaimed the young man, jumping to his feet. "I shall get my horse at once and meet you outside." With that, he hurried out of the room.

In need of a moment's relaxation, I filled my pipe and strolling out a side door gazed around the Tankard's enchanting garden. The rhododendron bushes were heavy with large purple blossoms and sweet peas and forget-me-nots bordered the pathway where I stood. What a fool for beauty am I!

Thomas soon appeared at the gate, leading his pretty black mare. I hastily joined him and we began our journey to Adderbury. It was a goodly pace from The Tankard's therefore; we didn't arrive at Cavendish Manor until late afternoon.

It was indeed a magnificent scene we came upon as we guided our mares onto the carriage path leading to the front entrance. On either side of us, there was an emerald green lawn spreading out around the manor to the rear area. In the center of the east lawn, there stood a sparkling fountain of Italian marble and thick shrubbery marked off the boundary line to a dense collection of trees in the background. A colorful profusion of flowers arranged in a circular design occupied the center of the west lawn. I noticed two large gray stone lions on high pedestals at the foot of the broad flagstone steps. One was on the left side and the other was on the right. These ferocious looking creatures stood majestically erect, glaring at us with cold unseeing eyes.

We dismounted, tying our horses. "Quite a breathtaking estate, wouldn't you say, Inspector?" Thomas remarked, deeply impressed.

"Indeed, it is my lad. I don't believe I've ever seen it's equal."

We moved up the steps onto a high pillared porch, then heard Lord Cavendish pull up on the graveled path behind us.

"Good afternoon, gentlemen." He called out cordially, dismounting a beautiful white stallion. Just then, a groom came along and led all the horses away. I eyed the man curiously. His Lordship soon joined us at the top of the steps and, I giving him my finest smile, introduced the lad, Thomas.

"I'm glad I returned in time to greet you, gentlemen," He said in quiet reserve, giving us a polite handshake.

Then, turning quickly, he opened the great front door, and we stepped into a large foyer. The butler, Merton, stood at stiff attention, taking our hats.

His Lordship beckoned us down a long corridor into a sumptuous drawing room, and my wandering eye took in every detail of beauty therein. Delicate Louis XIV furniture upholstered in gold satin graced the spacious room; and rich draperies of the same hue hung in deep folds on the tall arched windows. Precious antiques, which in my opinion would have compared favorably with those in the London museum, were placed here and there. I glanced sideways at Thomas. Seeing his blank expression, realized that he too was deeply impressed with all the splendor.

Lord Cavendish invited us to be seated, then walked over and closed the sliding doors opening into the corridor. Thomas sat down on one of the satin chairs, And I, seating myself on another, expected any moment to crash on the floor. But to my everlasting relief, it held me quite securely. His Lordship crossed the room and stood in front of us.

"Now then, gentlemen," he began seriously, "let us get down to the business at hand." He turned to me. "I take it, Inspector, you have enlightened your young assistant here as to the details of the case."

"Quite, your Lordship, quite," I answered, awaiting his next remark.

"Good!" he replied with a curt nod. "Now Inspector, I haven't disturbed a thing in my sitting room. All is the same as I found it yesterday morning. I believe this is the proper procedure."

"That is right, my Lord," I replied crisply, being thankful for his foresight in the matter.

The distinguished gentleman glanced towards the doorway for a moment, then said, "If you will follow me, I shall have Merton show you to your quarters. About 7 this evening, I shall come and escort you to my sitting room. I keep it locked at all times."

We rose obediently and followed him out into the hall. At this precise moment, I noticed a door at the far end close rather hurriedly. Thomas gave me a knowing glance.

In no time at all, Merton, the butler, escorted us up the stairway to the second floor. We found our room quite cheerful and sunny. The padded carpet underfoot was much to my liking, I must admit. Merton withdrew, and I watched him carefully as he left the room.

"Well, my lad, what do you think?" I asked, settling my bulk deep on a soft overstuffed sofa.

Thomas favored me with his infectious smile. "Inspector," he replied. "I think his Lordship is an elegant gentleman; and this fine Manor would be fit for our gracious Queen!"

"That is so, my lad." I murmured, casting an eye around our richly appointed room. Merton returned after a short time. Bringing us tea and sausage rolls, which pleased our palates immensely. Afterwards, I glanced at my timepiece and saw that it was only 6 p.m. So, the lad and I spent the next hour discussing famous criminal cases.

❦

At exactly 7 p.m., there came a soft rap on our door, and Lord Cavendish stepped into the room. He was richly attired in a frock coat suit of pearl gray broadcloth and a ruffled white shirt. A lavender silk cravat around his throat enhanced the costume. I was quite taken with his elegant appearance and realized I suffered greatly by comparison. He greeted us politely.

"Good evening gentlemen, I trust you've had tea."

Thomas and I nodded respectfully.

"Very good. Now I shall take you both to my sitting room."

We followed his lordship out the doorway into the wide luxurious corridor, advancing at a goodly pace toward the front of the manor. About halfway along, his lordship paused in front of a highly polished mahogany door and unlocked it.

The room we entered was lavishly furnished, and opposite the doorway, there was a great white marble fireplace, upon which sculptured cherubs and flowers abounded. A magnificent mirror in a gilded frame hung above the mantelpiece, reflecting the elegant interior of the room.

Lord Cavendish turned to us and said grimly. "Gentlemen, you will notice the state of things in here."

My eye traveled quickly over the papers strewn on the floor in front of an open wall safe, which was built into the east wall of the room. I walked over to it and removed an empty jewel case.

"Inspector, I must leave you now, as Lady Cavendish and I are expecting guests at any moment. I hope you will be successful in your search for clues." His lordship handed me the key to the sitting room, then left Thomas and me to ourselves.

"I would venture to say, inspector, that whoever stole the jewels must have been in a great haste." Remarked Thomas, as he moved slowly around the carpet with his torchlight.

"Quite so," I replied rather absently, holding my magnifying glass over the interior of the empty jewel case. In one corner there was a particle of fine powder.

After a moment or two, Thomas exclaimed excitedly. "I say! Inspector, look at this! It looks like a button from a lady's frock."

I quickly took the button from him and peered at it under my magnifying glass. The button was unusual in design, having a carved cherub face with sapphire eyes. Turning it over, I noticed that the shank was broken, as if it had been suddenly ripped off a garment. I dropped it neatly into my pocket for future reference, then, taking my penknife, scraped the powder out of the corner of the jewel case onto a small piece of paper which I carefully folded and deposited in my waistcoat pocket. This, I intended to examine more closely at a later date.

Having satisfied myself that the vault offered no other clue, I picked up the papers off the floor, replacing them therein. I also examined the lock of the safe door, finding it intact. In the meantime, Thomas had finished his painstaking inspection of the area, and I, feeling certain we had found all possible clues in the sitting room. Thought it might be to our advantage to inspect the immediate vicinity in the corridor. So, I unlocked the door quietly, and we stepped outside. At that moment, a pert little maid dashed past us down the corridor like a frightened doe and entered the front master bedroom.

"Well now, Thomas my lad, what do you make of that?" Said I, somewhat taken aback.

"Inspector," he replied firmly, "I would wager my last shilling the lassie was snooping around out here."

I agreed wholeheartedly with Thomas as I stared down the corridor, hoping the young woman would make a second appearance. We stood in silence for a while, then went on with the business at hand, completing our inspection with negative results. Realizing we could do no more for the present. I suggested returning to our quarters, and on the following day interrogate the servants in depth.

Later, in the privacy of our cozy room. I took the small ornate button out of my pocket and examined it under the glow of the oil lamp. I was convinced Thomas had uncovered an important clue. I examined it under my magnifier. The residue that I had scraped out of the corner of the jewel case. However, it proved to be only talcum powder dust and was of no significant importance.

Early the next morning, I immediately requested the presence of the servants in his Lordship's sitting room for questioning, and took my place there in front of the ornate fireplace about ten o'clock, with my young aide.

"My lad," I said to Thomas, "that little maid we saw in the corridor yesterday has stirred my curiosity. I believe I shall talk to her first. The others will remain out in the corridor and you will direct them inside one by one to be questioned. Moreover, I want you to take notes classifying each suspect so that I may study their personalities at my leisure."

We soon heard the servants' footsteps coming along the hall. I quickly motioned Thomas to greet them at the door. The dainty French maid was the first to enter, and she seemed extremely nervous as Thomas closed the door behind her and stood in front of it with his arms folded across his chest in a most author-itative manner. The young woman came forward reluctantly and stood facing me. I immediately put forth my first question.

"Tell me, Miss, what is your name?"

"Dorée Pané, sir," she replied timidly, fidgeting with her crisp, frilly apron.

"I see. Now, what are your duties in this house?"

"I am Lady Cavendeesh boudoir maid. I 'ave come not long from my 'ome, in Paree."

The young thing's command of the Kin's English left much to be desired, I must say!

"Have you ever been in this room before?" I queried, staring into her pretty face.

"No! No! Inspectair!" she cried.

"Did I not see you hurry past in the corridor, as my assistant and I emerged from this room last evening?" I watched her closely.

"Oui! Oui! But, I was not by thees doorway—I was on errand for my meestress, and I must 'urry."

I could tell by her agitated manner that she was not telling the whole truth. I pursued the question.

"Now Miss, are you not trying to mislead me? This particular room is of some interest to you, is it not?"

The dainty creature started to weep and stood, dabbing her large brown eyes with a wisp of a handkerchief, that gave out a most delicious scent of violets. This touched my soft heat, making me feel like an ogre belching hell-fire. Steeling myself, I went on with the interrogation.

"Now, Doree," said I in a gentler tone, "I want you to answer the next question in a truthful manner. Have you ever seen Lady Cavendish's pearls?"

Doree wavered slightly, then answered. "Oui, oui, but only around my lady's throat. Inspectair, I 'ave nevair touched them— I vow, by the blessed Virgin!"

Her tears fell copiously now, so I hastily dismissed her, and Thomas ushered in Giles, the valet.

As this person approached me, I realized I was in the presence of a cultured, well-trained individual. He was tall and immaculately groomed, and his dignified bearing was most certainly inbred. I looked at my notes, then addressed him thus.

"Your name is Giles?"

"Yes sir, that is correct." He replied.

"My man, how long have you been employed here as a valet?"

The fellow stared me straight in the eye and answered quite stiffly. "I have had the pleasure, sir, of serving his Lordship exactly three years and one fortnight."

"Very good." Said I, realizing that I had a proud and somewhat provoking fellow to deal with here. I inquired next, if he had had occasion to enter the sitting room alone on the evening before the pearls had been found missing.

"Inspector," the man answered disdainfully, drawing himself up to full height, "my presence heretofore in this room has always been in the company of Lord Cavendish." I concluded that he was telling the truth. Moreover, by this time I'd had my fill of his condescending attitude, so I waved him away quickly.

The next one to appear was the elderly butler, Merton. He was quite stooped and wore a mild, pleasant expression as he walked slowly across the room and stood facing me.

"Merton, my good fellow," I began, "How long have you been butler here at Cavendish Manor?"

"Ever since Lord Richard was an infant, sire." He replied quietly.

"I presume by that you mean Lord Cavendish?"

Merton's dim eyes softened considerably. "Yes indeed, sir."

"Now, my good fellow," I resume, "on the night of May fifteenth, did you enter this room for any purpose whatsoever?"

"My goodness, no, inspector," he answered straightforwardly, "Lord Richard keeps this room locked at all times as he is the only person who comes in here—although, I do believe Giles has accompanied him on occasion."

Well! Thought I, the valet's story is confirmed right enough. As far as I could tell, the old butler seemed quite innocent of any wrongdoing. Therefore, I kindly told him he could go. He smiled and nodded at me in a most respectful manner, then left the room. I interrogated Mrs. Bean, the cook, and Bertie, the groom next. Neither one, in my best judgment, was involved in the case. So, that left only Caldwell, the gardener, yet to be questioned. I directed Thomas to show the man in.

I have, at times in my long career, come in contact with certain individuals who present such an obstinate attitude that it takes a great deal of persuasion on my part prying loose any information at all. My intuition told me Caldwell was one of these, as I watched him sullenly approach me. I wasted no time.

"I take it your name is Caldwell?" I asked.

"That's the moniker I've 'ad for over forty years." The fellow replied in a most uncivil manner. I went on.

"I believe you are the gardener here. Am I correct?"

"You can believe what you want. I don't care." He returned flippantly. My patience was wearing quite thin at this point.

"Now sir," I continued, assuming a stern front, "I expect you to give me a sensible answer to my next question. Have you ever been in this room before?"

The rascal's insolent expression hardened, and he thrust his right hand quickly into his coat pocket. I took this to be a threatening gesture, so, for a moment, I was on the defensive. Then he relaxed, and with a cynical grin spreading across his surly face, answered my question.

"Inspector, you're balmy in the 'ead. What business would I 'ave up 'ere, anyway?"

The insulting remark about my head ruffled me to no end, and I became quite hot under the collar.

"My man!" I exclaimed angrily, "your rudeness is absolutely uncalled for! Now, just where were you on the night of May fifteenth?" I was quite stern.

"Just like I told you, inspector, minding my own business." He replied slyly. His sharp, beady eyes stared right through me.

"That is quite sufficient!" I sputtered, turning my back on him. I heard the scoundrel laugh sarcastically as he crossed the room and went out the door. This individual, thought I, would be kept under strict surveillance, or my name wasn't Inspector Lemont.

After Caldwell left the room, I walked over and joined Thomas at the doorway.

"Thomas," said I, in a most serious tone of voice, "I want you to watch that fellow closely, and report any suspicious action on his part to me immediately."

"I shall do that, sir," my young aide returned soberly. He paused, then added, "Do you know, inspector, I had the most peculiar feeling that the fellow was laughing at us."

"Well, my lad, let me assure you that the scoundrel didn't amuse me in the least, and it may happen that we shall have the last laugh after all," I replied, somewhat smugly.

We then went out into the corridor, and I locked the sitting-room door. Thomas turned on his heel and trailed Caldwell down the rear stairs, and I descended to the first floor and went outside onto the wide front porch.

It was one of those delightful spring days when mother nature, in all her sweet glory, shimmers with ecstasy. A gentle breeze wafted the scent of lilacs and honeysuckle from the garden. As I stood drinking in the beauty and the wonder of it all, my shape eye caught the petite form of the French maid moving slowly along a leafy pergola, which led from the side entrance of the Manor to the garden.

Being most anxious to question the pert lassie again, I hurried down the front steps, and in no time came up beside her in the cool interior of the pergola. She glanced up at me in a startled manner, and her tear-stained cheeks told me that my interrogation an hour ago had disturbed her greatly. I had no intention of brow-beating the comely you miss, however; I felt certain that she was withholding vital information regarding the missing pearls. And it was my duty to see if this was true. So, I took her by the arm and guided her to an arbor at the end of the leafy walk. We sat down together in the secluded spot, and I gently put forth this question.

"My dear young lady. I have a feeling you haven't told me everything you know about Lady Cavendish's pearls—isn't that so?"

The young lass hung her head, and, much agitated, started twisting her pretty apron into a knot in her lap. I waited patiently for her to calm down. In a moment, she straightened up and, glancing around quickly, cried out.

"Oh! Inspector, I cannot hold thees secret anymore- I will tell you what I know."

Turning her dark velvety eyes on me, she continued hurriedly. "Some days back, I was taking promenade in thees same place. I lak to come here when I have nothing to do. When I was seeting here, I got very sleepy but then, I hear voices close outside. I listen, then peek through lattice, and there I see meestress and that man gardener talking low, but I hear what they say!

Meestess say, 'Don't worry, I shall get them for you tonight after they are locked up.' Then that man, he growl lak big bear and say, 'Don't you make me wait or you know what will happen.' Then he turned around and walked far away, and my poor lady, she stand for long time blanch white, then she go in house."

The dainty little creature's face clouded. "Inspector, I don't lak that man Caldwell," she continued thoughtfully. "He bad man- one time I hear him say he keel cook, just because she move some of his plants outside the house. He shouted at cook, 'I keel you old woman, if you ever touch any of my plants again!' Then he shook his feest just lak this." Doree held up her pretty little fist, by way of demonstration, and shook it fiercely.

I was most thankful for gaining this information, but was mightily shocked hearing of Lady Cavendish's entanglement with Caldwell. I surmised that blackmail was the key issue here. All of a sudden. The pert little maid jumped to her feet and peered anxiously out of the lattice framework. Standing up beside her, I too put an eye to one of the vents and saw Caldwell in the distance, busily pruning in the arbor. I placed my hand lightly on the young lady's shoulder and said soothingly, "Missy, fear not, I'm certain Caldwell is far out of earshot."

Doree nodded, yet a shadow of doubt clouded her pretty face. Clearing my throat, I stood gazing at her for quite a spell. What a delectable little creature she was, thought I, with her soft doe eyes and alabaster skin, setting off a mass of cloudy dark hair peeking out around her frilly white cap. Her appealing loveliness fairly melted my crusty old heart- ah! Thought I, sweet youth! Sweet youth! Where art thou?

Jolting myself back to earth, I thanked Doree heartily for her co-operation, asking her to report to me anything suspicious she might encounter as she went about her duties; and then, somewhat reluctantly, released her, my eye following her down the pergola into the house.

Encourage with the progress I'd made in the case. Up to this point, I strolled out of the arbor onto the vast green lawn and followed a circular pathway that brought me to the front entrance of the manor. Caldwell was busily engaged clipping a thick hedge, and as I passed by, he leered at me, however; I took no notice of him whatsoever, for I was confident my trusty young aide, Thomas, was secreted somewhere nearby observing Caldwell's every move.

Upon entering the house, I proceeded up the stairway to our quarters on the second floor. Searing myself at a table by the window, I withdrew the small round button from my pocket and examined it a second time. I asked myself; had this been accidentally ripped off Lady Cavendish's frock while she was removing the pearls from the safe? As I pondered this, Thomas entered the room in a great flurry.

"Inspector," he reported breathlessly, "that ruffian, Caldwell, mistreated the pretty little French maid just now!" From my point of observation, I noticed Doree emerge from the side door of the manor and go slowly around to the front of the house to join Caldwell.

Thomas's youthful expression turned quite serious, as he continued with his report thus. "Inspector, I'll wager this was a prearranged meeting. For instantly, there was a sharp exchange of words between them, which I could not make out. Then suddenly, the young lady riled up and started stomping her foot on the ground, shaking her head vigorously. Then, to my utter dismay, I saw Caldwell raise his hand and strike Doree most cruelly across the cheek! I had to restrain myself from immediately attacking the cad."

The lad's fine blue eyes flashed indignantly, and I saw at once that his delicate sense of chivalry was injured.

I turned this new development over in my mind, becoming, by the moment, more and more interested in the petite French maid. Was her tale of Lady Cavendish and Caldwell fictitious after all? Did Doree have a subtle part in this affair? And furthermore, what was the relationship between her and Caldwell? "Thomas, my lad," I said quietly, "Did Caldwell and Doree enter the house together?"

"No sir, they did not," Thomas replied hastily, "I had my eye on them all the time. Caldwell, the confounded scoundrel, grasped the poor maid's arm and dragged her to the east side of the steps, forcing her to stand still. Then he bent down and loosened a section of cement at the base of the lion, removing a small parcel wrapped in white paper and upon opening it, gazed intently at its contents for some time."

"Fine detection, my lad," I exclaimed, patting his sturdy young shoulder. I then acquainted him with the maid's account of Lady Cavendish and Caldwell's meeting, and when I finished, I asked him what his deductions were so far. Thomas frowned, and hooking his thumbs in his waistcoat pocket (quite professionally) walked back and forth in front of me, his keen young mind working like clockwork. I smiled benignly, awaiting his response.

"Inspector," he broke out, at last, "I'm beginning to suspect Doree and Caldwell are romantically attached, and he, wishing to gain possession of the pearls, which in all likelihood he had spied around her Ladyship's throat at one time or another, wheeled Doree into obtaining them. And, I believe Caldwell keeps the jewels secreted in the base of the lion in readiness for his and the French maid's hasty departure which incidentally, may occur at any moment.

"Thomas, I do believe you have hit it right on the nose. Well, we will have our work cut out for us, eh what? However, my lad, the button you unearthed on the sitting room floor is a vital piece of evidence in our favor."

Thomas nodded with a wide grin. I thought things over for a moment. Then continued. "Now, I believe it would be to our advantage if by some means you could gain admittance to the maid's bedchamber, and thereby examine her wardrobe. I have a hunch you will find a costume with the same type button missing. What do you think?"

"That's a brilliant suggestion, inspector," Thomas replied, his eyes lighting up, "I shall go immediately and find Merton the butler. He will be helpful, I'm sure."

I grinned at him. "Go now lad, and see what you can find." Thomas hurried out the door, and I, moving over to the tall arched window, stood gazing down on the magnificent marble fountain on the east lawn. Just then, a soft rap came upon my door, and Lord Cavendish entered the room.

"Inspector," he said, "please excuse the intrusion, but I must ask if you have any concrete evidence as yet?" His fine sensitive features were drawn with deep concern.

"Yes, I have indeed, your Lordship," I replied politely. I acquainted him then with the discussion I had had with the French maid and her astounding accusation concerning Lady Cavendish, informing him also of the event of the broken button. "We have a suspicion, your Lordship," I said smoothly, "that the missing necklace may be secreted in the base of the east lion at the foot of the front steps."

His Lordship whirled around angrily. Before he could say anything, I went on to tell him of Doree meeting Caldwell, and their mysterious actions in front of the house.

"The miserable pair!" his Lordship cried vehemently, "how dare they implicate my wife in their foul schemes. I shall dismiss them instantly! I see my suspicions regarding Caldwell, has born fruit. It would please me greatly to thrash the ruffian to within an inch of his life!" Lord Cavendish, extremely upset, clenched his hands into quite sturdy fists, which I would not have cared to come in contact with my jaw.

"Please, your Lordship," I countered, "I beg of you, do not act hastily. I admit that this is a deplorable situation; nevertheless, it is imperative that Thomas and I proceed cautiously, and under-cover, in this case, otherwise, we cannot hope to attain the clinching evidence required to bring the culprits to justice."

Lord Cavendish's demeanor softened as he gazed down at me steadily. "Yes, yes," he replied, "you are quite correct; I under-stand perfectly." Then lapsing into silence for a few moments, he strode back and forth in front of me, then stopped and said, "Inspector Lemont, the matter is entirely in your hands, and I shall await developments. However, the sooner Caldwell and his French accomplice are incarcerated, the better I shall like it."

I then informed his Lordship I had directed Thomas to search the maid's wardrobe for a possible missing button. He nodded approvingly, then turning on his heel, left the room. What a fine gentleman! Thought I, my eye following his broad shoulders out of the door.

I walked over to the sofa and sat down, awaiting Thomas's report. I had decided that if his search of Doree's bedchamber proved fruitful, I would immediately summon the girl and keep her under lock and key on the strength of the evidence presented. The time passed slowly, and I became a trifle bored, so, I rose and wandered around the small room searching for reading matter, but found only one or two romantic novels which, at the moment, interested me not at all. Suddenly, young

Thomas burst into the room with a black satin frock draped over his arm.

"Here it is, inspector!" he exclaimed, his merry eyes sparkling with excitement, "there's a button missing right here, see?" He pointed at a few loose threads at the throat line. I took the garment from him and carried it over to the window, Removing the cherub button from my pocket, I compared it with those on the frock, finding to my satisfaction that it was identical in design and size all having cherub faces with sapphire eyes.

"Thomas," said I firmly, "we now have the evidence we need. I shall go at once to Lord Cavendish's sitting room; meanwhile, you go and inform that French maid I wish to see her there immediately."

Out in the corridor, I walked briskly toward the front of the house with the black satin frock tucked under my arm while Thomas hurried in the opposite direction and down the rear stairs in search of Doree.

Once inside the sitting room, I took a position in front of the ornate fireplace and deposited the accusing black frock underneath a richly carved table which stood nearby. After about a quarter of an hour, according to my timepiece, there came a timid knock upon the door and in came the pert little maid wearing an expression of woeful anxiety. I bade her sit down I began sternly.

"Now, my girl, let me have the truth and nothing but the truth." Doree's frightened doe-like eyes looked up into mine.

"Inspectaire, I 'ave told you the truth."

I put my hands behind my back and stood staring down at her. She moved restlessly around in her chair, giving me a pleading glance every now and then. I suddenly thrust the cherub button under her nose.

"Have you ever seen this button before?" I was determined to wear her down this time.

"Non, non, inspectaire!" she cried in quick defense,

Reaching down under the table, I drew forth the satin frock and held it up in front of her bulging eyes.

"Young lady," I fired back, "is this not a piece of your wearing apparel?" She began to sob bitterly. However, I was not going to be taken in a second time. "Tut, tut, Miss," I continued ruthlessly, "let us not have any more tears. I want you to examine this garment and tell me if there is a button missing anywhere."

Doree reluctantly took hold of the frock, looking closely where each button was sewed on, her pretty face pale as a sheet. After a while, she mumbled shakily. "A button ees missing from the neckline, inspectaire."

"That is entirely correct, my girl," said I somewhat pompously. "Now Miss," I continued, "I want you to take this button I have in my hand, and compare it with those on the garment. Are they not all the same?"

Doree took the button and fumbled around with it; and in the face of overwhelming evidence confronting her, flushed with guilt and embarrassment. I was getting impatient with this little suspect.

"Doree, do you still deny that this is your garment?" I persisted; I peered into her face.

Quickly covering her face with her hands, she sobbed, "Oui, oui, inspectaire, eet is mine."

I hesitated a moment, then continued more kindly. "Now Doree, I'm waiting to hear the whole truth about this affair."

Meanwhile, Thomas had slipped into the sitting room unnoticed and was standing in the doorway with his arms folded across his chest. Then, quite suddenly, the young Miss clutched my arm. Staring up at me with those great brown eyes of hers.

"Inspectaire, he made me do it!" She declared frantically, her tears splashing on my coat sleeve.

"My girl, who made you do it?" I asked.

Doree brushed away her tears with the back of her hand. "That man Caldwell, 'ee's the one," she replied in a quick manner. Inspectaire, 'ee wanted my lady's pearls very bad, and 'ee made me get them for 'eem." The pretty little thing started to tremble as she continued her confession hurriedly, one word tumbling over the other.

"That night in my lady's boudoir. I watch her take off the pearls and hand them to master Cavendish to lock up. So, after my lady go to sleep in her bedroom, I sneak in there and open French Door and step outside onto the balcony, then I crawl along ledge to master's sitting-room window, I peek inside and see master sitting at 'ees desk examining pearls, then I watch 'eem get up and open safe." Doree stopped to dab her eyes, and taking a deep breath, continued her interesting tale.

"Inspectaire, it was so easy! Master just press a small panel on the wall, and the safe door, she fly open just lak that! I knew I could do same, so, I wait long time outside window until master leave room, then I go inside and get pearls right away."

I rather got the impression the young culprit was gloating, for she stood looking up at me in a bold manner, a smug smile playing around the corners of her cupid-bow mouth.

"Young woman, where are the pearls now?" I demanded.

Doree shrugged her shoulders in typical bourgeois fashion. "I geeve them to Caldwell." What a sly little minx she was!

Thomas and I exchanged glances. I beckoned him, instructing him to escort the girl to her bedchamber and lock her in, then report back to me. Thomas took the French maid's arm somewhat gingerly and led her out the sitting-room door.

I devised a plan of action thus. My young aide and I would take a position. That night, in the shrubbery near the east lion, I finally concluded that Caldwell and the French maid had a violent disagreement over an equal sharing of the loot; therefore, it stood to reason that Caldwell's first act would be to retrieve the pearls as quickly as possible, then make his escape under the cover of darkness. However, the well-laid plans of mice and men often go awry, thought I, as I paced to and fro flapping my coat-tails behind me.

In a short time, Thomas joined me, reporting that Doree had cursed Caldwell all the way up to her bedchamber door, and he had been shocked to the core at her choice of foul words.

"Inspector," he said, a dark frown creasing his smooth forehead, "one certainly cannot judge a book by its cover, can one?"

I laughed. "No, indeed my lad; and as you progress further in this business, you'll appreciate that fact more and more. Come now, we must go and inform his Lordship." I closed and locked the sitting-room door softly behind us, and Thomas and I made our way along the corridor and down the magnificent stairway to the foyer.

Lady Cavendish, coming out of the drawing-room at that moment, graciously approached us with a kindly greeting.

"I presume you are Inspector Lemont?" she asked, giving me a sweet smile.

"Yes, your Ladyship, that is correct, and this young man is my aide, Thomas Malachee." I replied, returning her smile. She nodded to Thomas, then inquired if we had any information regarding the missing pearls.

I stood gazing at her ladyship in awe and admiration, being stuck instantly with her regal bearing. She wore her blond hair coiled high above her white brow, like a golden crown, and in her velvet gown of soft purple, she appeared every inch a queen. Lady Cavendish was indeed the most beautiful woman I had ever laid eyes on, and I, who never failed to appreciate loveliness whenever I found it, envied his Lordship to no end. Small wonder then, his deep emotion and anger against Caldwell for causing Lady Cavendish even a moment's concern. I shook myself awake, so to speak, and got to the matter at hand, revealing Doree's confession and the incident in front of the house.

Her Ladyship was horrified. "Oh! My goodness, inspector," she gasped, "surely my Doree is not involved in all this. She came to me with the finest of references." Her gorgeous lavender-blue eyes anxiously searched my pudgy countenance, make my senses reel.

"I'm afraid she is, your Ladyship," said I, looking away quickly.

Lady Cavendish shook her head sadly as she led Thomas and me into the drawing-room. His Lordship, entering a rear door, came hurriedly toward us. "Do sit down, gentlemen," he said cordially. "I suspect you have something to report."

Eyeing an overstuffed chair nearby, I dropped in it heavily and almost toppled a small pedestal upon which rested a priceless jade figurine. I broke out in cold perspiration, chiding myself inwardly for being such a clumsy ox. My gracious clients took no heed of the incident.

"Well, inspector?" His Lordship gazed expectantly in my direction.

Clearing my throat in a professional manner, I then acquainted him with Doree's confession and my plan of action.

"Rest assured your Lordship, Caldwell will be apprehended, and the pearls restored to you this very night."

Lord Cavendish walked over to his beautiful lady and placed his hand on her arm. "Very good, inspector. We shall await you in my sitting room."

I reached into my pocket and gave him the sitting room key.

That evening after twilight, Thomas and I stepped out the side entrance of the manor and make our way along the pergola to the arbor and waited. The night was soft and balmy, and busy fireflies sparked a zig-zag pattern in the gloom, and a scent of wild-roses mingled with the earthy aroma of new mown grass permeated the air, filling me with the heady flavor of springtime. But my fine young Thomas, standing stiff and alert at my side, concerned himself only with the matter at hand.

After a while we noticed the rosy glow of a lantern bobbing its way along the side pathway toward the front of the house, and we soon recognized Caldwell's dim outline. He stopped near the east lion and set the lantern down on the ground.

"Come, Thomas!" I whispered, grabbing hold of his arm. We retraced our steps along the pergola and cautiously followed the pathway making certain we stayed close to the thick shrubbery, out of sight. Reaching the end of the pathway, we halted and stood observing Caldwell's every move. Bending over, he loosened a section of masonry at the base of the lion, then, placing his hand into a small space, withdrew a white paper parcel, and opened it; and in the flow of the lantern, a crooked smile spread across his evil-looking features as he held the gleaming Cavendish pearls up in front of his beady eyes.

"Now! Thomas, now!" I whispered urgently, instantly pulling forth my firearm from under my waistcoat. I was prepared for any untoward action on Caldwell's part. We crossed the lawn hurriedly and came face to face with the rascal.

"Don't make a move! You are under arrest!" I commanded tersely. Caldwell, taken by surprise, straightened up and glared at me wildly. I snatched the pearls out of his greedy hands and dropped them into my coat pocket. Thomas quickly closed in and clasped handcuffs on his wrists, then we marched the ruffian along the pathway and into the side entrance of the manor.

Caldwell soon found his voice. "Inspector 'ow in 'ell, did ye do it? No, I salute ye, I do. Say! Did the little French give me away?" He gave me a sardonic grin, muttering something under his breath as we steered him up the stairway to Lord Cavendish's sitting room. I took no notice of the man, whatsoever.

His Lordship scowled at Caldwell when we entered the room. I gently laid the precious pearls on the table in front of him and watched the little drama with interest.

"Well, Caldwell!" he rasped, "What excuse do you have to offer for your abominable conduct?"

Caldwell, his beady little eyes darting here and there, brazenly retorted. "I don't 'ave to give excuses to nobody, that's what!"

His Lordship stiffened. "I ought to give you a thorough thrashing! Right here and now, you miserable cad! How dare you implicate my wife in this affair! Take him away!" He turned on his heel and walked over to Lady Cavendish, who stood serene and pale, gazing out the window.

I nodded toward the doorway, and Thomas, catching my meaning, guided Caldwell out of the room and closed the door. At this, his Lordship turned around to me and came forward hand outreached.

"Excellent work inspector," he complimented. "Rest assured, I shall forward you a generous fee."

I thanked him on behalf of Thomas and myself, then bowing politely to her ladyship, took my leave.

Thomas lad was standing outside in the corridor with a firm hold on Caldwell's arm. I instructed him to take Caldwell to the maid's room and keep them both under guard, I then handed him my firearm, which I'm sure made a deep impression on our prisoner for he slouched down the corridor beside Thomas, meek as could be.

I hurried down the stairs and out the front door. Mounting Dolly at the foot of the steps, I started off at a good clip toward Dartma. When I reached my destination, I immediately notified Constable Spears, and together we acquired the conveyance reserved for criminals, and sped back to Cavendish Manor, making the arrest.

On the following afternoon, my helpful young aide and I sat enjoying a glass of ale in the Tankards refreshment room.

"Well, inspector," Thomas remarked proudly, "we've solved another case, eh what?"

I laughed. "Yes, my lad, that we have, and no doubt there shall be others coming our way before long."

Thomas stood up, a merry twinkle in his eye. "Then, sir, I shall await your call."

I rose up beside him, slapping him on the back. "Thomas, my dear chap, you are indispensable." I meant every word of it. The lad favored me with a wide boyish grin, then walked away.

Strolling out the door to the roadside, I tweaked Dolly's velvety ear and whispered, "Well old girl, shall we go home now?" and the faithful creature seeming to understand my words, whinnied and bobbed her head up and down as I climbed in the saddle.

ONCE FRESH AND NEW

❧ I ❧

SOUTH CAROLINA 1890

The surrey swayed lazily from side to side on the hot dusty road. Melissa held the reins limply in her small black-laced gloved hands. The glaring sun bore down on the fringed surrey top, and a suffocating breeze fanned Melissa's heart-shaped face like a blast from an open furnace. Her pancake hat was askew on top of her chestnut curls and she twisted and turned on the carriage seat trying to get comfortable. After a while, she guided Dimity off the road and brought her to a halt under the cool shade of two tall elm trees and leaned back on the hot leather seat with a sigh of relief. Opening her black-beaded bag she took out a small lace handkerchief and mopped her wet forehead and then closed her eyes to relax a while. Dimity, eager to be off again, started dancing around. Melissa sat up and said, "You crazy ninny, ya all quiet yourself, ya hear," she gave the reins a sharp jerk and Dimity rolled her big eyes and snorted, then settled down nibbling on a tuft of grass.

Flinging the reins aside, Melissa stared down at her new pink-silk dress. The pert black-velvet bows attached to the beautifully draped skirt, still looked stylish and elegant and so did her pretty black-lace parasol and matching half-gloves. She thought she looked mighty good when she left the house that morning, but just look at her now! Making a wry face she slid down on the seat and folded her arms, her eyes staring straight ahead. Having been elected recording secretary for the Batesburg Charity Club, about six months ago, it was Melissa's duty at each monthly meeting to rise and read the minutes. As luck would have it, when she stood up on the platform this morning, her over-sized black-lace bustle tore loose from its moorings and hung down behind her knees like a bundle of wash, and that was not all, for when she hurriedly stepped down from the platform she stumbled and fell into the arms of a tall blond man. Grinning broadly, the man asked her if she had hurt herself, Melissa just stared at him then fled down the aisle and out of the meeting hall door. Angry with herself and everybody else, Melissa half-rose on the seat and ripped the offending bustle off the back of her dress and threw it out on the road, "That darn miss fancy-britches," she muttered, "ah sure will let her know what ah think about her dressmaking!" Soured and disgusted, Melissa took up the reins and drove home.

Clay Hampton stood the wide white-pillared porch of Highacres watching his attractive daughter guide the surrey around the winding driveway and come to a stop at the foot of the steps. Wondering about her glum expression, he went slowly down the steps and fastened the reins to the hitching post, and helped her down from the surrey. The stately old mansion towered high wide and handsome above them. Its broad white facade, lofty gables, and tall narrow windows green-shuttered against the sun had sheltered three generations of Hamptons. During the Civil war, Highacres was one of the first southern plantations to fall under a Yankee domination, and only by great-uncle Beau Hampton's smooth-talking a Yankee captain telling him that he was a Union sympathizer, did the grand old mansion escape burning to the ground. Uncle Beau's oval-framed likeness hung proudly over the white-marble fireplace in the drawing room and on entering the room, one's eyes were immediately drawn to the powerful hard-bitten features and defiant black eyes. When Melissa was a little girl, she would often go into the drawing room and stand gazing up at Uncle Beau's picture wondering if he knew all that was going on in the house.

Melissa stood at the foot of the steps holding her open parasol behind her. Giving his daughter an odd look, Clay moved slowly around her and said, "Lisse my pet, you sure look mighty comical holding your parasol that way," he paused, grinning, "did you lose your bustle?" A mischievous gleam came in his mild gray eyes as he circled her again, "Well now, I guess you did because I don't see it anywhere."

Melissa gave him a petulant glance. "Daddy," she replied soberly, "ahm in no mood to be teased... it's not a bit funny." Her lip quivered and tears came in her eyes.

"Now, now, sugar, don't take on, you just tell daddy all about it," soothed Clay putting his arm around her slim shoulder and leading her up the steps to the front door. When they entered the dim lofty foyer, Melissa's high-pitched voice rang out loudly as she related all that had happened to her that morning at the meeting hall. She told her father she would never get over it as long as she lived. Clay understood her embarrassment but told her that a dress was only a dress, and said that acting lady-like was far more important. Had she controlled her temper in front of those ladies at the Charity meeting, he asked.

Somewhat hurt, Melissa eyed her father. "Daddy," she returned loftily, "ah behaved as best I could with those awful things happening to me one after the other... but if it hadn't been for that man catching hold of me when I tripped off the platform, ahm sure I would have let out a cuss word or two..."

Clay quickly put his finger to his lips, interrupting her. "Hush up sugar," he said, "you don't want your mamma to overhear you, do you?" No, indeed not! Thought Melissa, one upset was enough. Clay patted her arm and whispered affectionately, "Run along now and change that raggedy looking dress and," he added, "be sure you have a pleasant look on your pretty face before you come downstairs." He gently shoved her toward the stairway and stood watching her slowly climbing the stairs dragging her black-lace parasol behind her.

"Did I hear Melissa's voice just now?" Luella Hampton's soft even tone came from the drawing-room doorway. She stood tall and willowy in the door frame in a modish dark-green taffeta dress. Her shinning dark-brown hair was pulled back off her marble-like face in a fashionable chignon and her overly large green eyes were two deep unfathomable pools. Luella's bearing was that of the old south with great plantations and negro slaves as a way of life. Clay had married her twenty years ago and brought her home to Highacres from Savannah, deeply proud of her stunning beauty and genteel background. It was true that Luella's family was recognized far and wide as the cream of Savannah aristocracy. Her mother's brother Daniel McCombe, a former governor of South Carolina, distinguished himself bravely in the battle of Bull Run, and her father Lange De Mott served as Major General under General Lee and died gallantly for the cause.

Proud of her own breeding, Luella had taken Melissa in hand soon after she entered her teen years training her as best she could to become a lady. She abhorred Melissa's loud sharp tone of voice and boisterous ways and reminded her that unless she calmed down and watched herself she would never catch a husband. Melissa had solemnly listened and with a sigh wondered if her mother had ever had any real fun in her life. Luella was very difficult to live with at times with her painfully proper air and stiff outlook on life and more than that, she had no sense of humor whatsoever; she lived by her own rock-bound convictions and if one happened to express an opinion of his own, Luella would stop him cold with those enormous green eyes of hers. Still and all, Melissa adored her gorgeous mother and stood in awe of her.

Clay turned and looked at his wife. Even after all these years his heart leaped at the sight of her. Walking over to the doorway a smile on his round pleasant face, he said, "Yes, Melissa just came in. She's gone upstairs to change her dress."

Luella's eyebrows went up as she glanced at the hall clock. "I wonder why she is home so early I thought that charity meeting didn't close until three o'clock."

Clay grinned and replied, "Oh well, you know how Melissa is. It's mighty hot out today, so I guess she just decided to come home and cool off a bit."

"I know you are covering up for her, Clay," returned Luella lightly, 'but never mind, I'll just see for myself." Gathering up her green silk skirts, she crossed the foyer and climbed the stairs to Melissa's room at the end of the hall. Tapping lightly on the door once or twice, she waited for an answer, then entered the dim pink and white bedroom. They heavy dark-green blinds were drawn down to the window sill and Melissa lay sprawled on the bed, her eyes closed tight. Luella calmly stepped over the pink-silk dress lying in a heap in the middle of the floor, and sat down on the edge of the bed. "Melissa," she said, "why are you home so early?" It was though she was speaking to a ten-year-old child.

Melissa opened her round hazel eyes and stared at her mother. She wished she had stayed at the meeting, for her mother was uncanny smelling out trouble. "Melissa, why did you come home so early?" asked Luella again, in a soft, firm tone. Sitting up,

Melissa poured out the whole miserable story, not that she wanted to, but, Luella was Luella and one always went along with her. With her knees up under her chin, she waited for her mother to say something. Luella rose from the bed and went over and picked up the torn dress and examined it frontwards and backwards her expression calm.

"Really, Melissa," she said at last, "you tend to dramatize minor things, don't you? As far as I can see, you had a simple unavoidable accident not worth carrying on about, and as for your dress, it can easily be repaired." Luella held up the back of the dress and glanced around the room. "Where is the bustle?" she quietly asked.

Shrugging her dainty shoulders, Melissa replied, "I threw the cussed thing away, oh mother," she moaned, drawing her mouth down like a child about to cry. "I've never been so embarrassed in all my life and when I tripped off that darn platform in front of a strange man, it finished me for the day."

"You needn't use vulgar words to explain yourself, Melissa. It is not ladylike," said Luella as she crossed the room to the clothes closet and hung up the dress. Coming back again, she stood over Melissa and informed her that she had invited uncle Louis and aunt Sara Hampton and their two girls, Mary Joe and Linda May, to dinner. "You know they always arrive early," she said. "So, I will expect you downstairs in half an hour."

Melissa gave her mother a dark frown and pulled herself up on the side of the bed. "Of all days to invite them over!" Melissa's voice rose excitedly. "Why can't I just stay up here out of the way —all Mary Joe ever talks about is her stupid music teacher, and it bores me silly listening to her. I swear she's in love with the man."

"That is none of your business, Melissa, and I do not care to argue about your coming downstairs, furthermore, keep your voice down. Mary Joe is your first cousin." Luella reminded her firmly, "and she deserves your respect, like it or not. I only wish you were as accomplished and refined as Mary Joe and that goes for Linda May too. By the way, did you know that Linda May wants to study medicine?"

Melissa gaped at her mother. "Study medicine?" she scoffed, "why, that's the most ridiculous thing I've ever heard of—who would go to a female doctor?"

"Lots of people would," replied Luella lightly. "I once knew of a lady doctor in Savannah who had a very successful practice."

"Well, it sounds idiotic to me," returned Melissa flippantly, "lady doctor, my hat! Linda May must be crazy."

Heaving a sigh, Luella turned and walked over to the doorway. "Your father and I will wait in the drawing room," she said, as she quietly left the room.

Sara Hampton wedged her ample figure in between her two daughters on the carriage seat, complaining about the hot weather. Her pudgy face streamed perspiration down the front of her lace jabot and a cameo brooch under her chin. Holding a dark-blue silk parasol high over her white leghorn hat adorned with satin ribbons and red cherries, she remarked grumpily, "It's just too hot to go anyplace today. I wish I hadn't accepted Luella's invitation to dinner." She smoothed the folds of her figured-silk dress over her fat knees and looked sourly at her husband's back as he picked up the reins and started off down the driveway.

Mary Joe turned and looked at her mother's puffy profile. "Don't worry mamma," she placated, "aunt Luella will find a cool spot to serve dinner. You know she always considers her guests' comfort." Mary Joe turned her head away and drank in the beauty of the blue mountain ridges far off in the distance. Their enthralling splendor touched her deeply. As they drove by the old Jefferson place, her bright blue eyes scanned the fallow cotton fields. Too bad Jeffersons lost everything and moved away, she thought idly. They had been pappa's next-door neighbors as long as she could remember. About two years ago they had sold out to some northern people, but as yet, there was nobody living in the old fifteen-room house on the hill.

Sarah's gruff voice broke her train of thought, saying, "For goodness' sake, Mary Joe, can't you move over a bit and give me more room? I just know I'll die of this terrible heat."

Leaning back on the seat, Mary Hoe inched away from her mother's sweaty body. "Is that better?" she asked. She got only a grunt for an answer. It did not take much to upset Sara Hampton. Hot weather. Cold weather, whatever. Sara complained about everything. Her husband, Louie, said she was born protesting the world and there was nothing one could do about it.

Linda May reached for her mother's hand. "Just try to relax, dear. If you take a few deep breaths now and then, you'll begin to feel a lot cooler," she advised softly.

Sara glared at her youngest daughter. "Thank you doctor, why don't you try it and see if it works?" Linda May gave her mother a tolerant smile and busied herself with her own thoughts.

It was about three o'clock in the afternoon when they arrived at Highacres. Clay greeted them on the wide shady porch and led them inside the house out of the heat. "Whew! What a day! I must say, I feel a lot cooler in here." Sara remarked as she took off her over-trimmed hat and set it on the hall table. "Where is Luella?" she asked, motioning the girls to remove their hats.

Clay answered with a quick smile, "She's waiting for us in the drawing room."

"Leave it to Luella to stay cool and unruffled on a day like this. I wish I could be like her," sighed Sara. "But one doesn't expect a frog to turn into a butterfly."

Sara's raucous laughter filled the hall. She thought she had said something very funny. Melissa, sitting on a red-velvet sofa in the drawing room, her pale-green voile dress falling demurely over her knees, shuddered at the sound of her aunt Sara's rough voice out in the hall. She despised the woman, but knew enough to treat her politely. Luella had seen to that. Her eye on the doorway, she watched them all trail after her father into the drawing room, and sit down. She admired the indigo-blue silk dress that Mary Joe had on. The color made her cousin's beautiful blue eyes sparkle like dew and with her honey blonde hair; she looked for all the world, like a delicate china doll. Melissa was envious of Mary Joe's looks even though she got on her nerves chattering about that music teacher of hers. She glanced at Linda May standing talking quietly to Luella. The ugly dark-red dress she wore seemed to match her dull flat features. Linda May is going to be as coarse and fat as her mother, mused Melissa. Spotting aunt Sara coming her way, she force a smile.

"My dear Melissa, how lovely and cool you look," gushed Sara, bending down to kiss her cheek. Melissa almost gagged, whiffing stale rose cologne. Sara's broad pink face beamed as she playfully flipped a stray curl on Melissa's forehead, "I declare you have the loveliest chestnut hair I've ever seen," she said, in her deep throaty voice. "Don't you dare dye it!" she laughed. "I dyed my hair once, and it turned an awful shade of green... your uncle Louis was going to put me in a circus and call me the green-haired monster." Sarah laughed harder. "Just a joke, of course," Uncle Louie frowned at his wife over his glasses.

Sara plumped down on the sofa beside Melissa and started prattling about Mary Joe's music. "You wouldn't believe how much Mary Joe has improved since that good-looking Mr. Devon came on the scene," she confided. "You can bet your life I got the best piano teacher around these parts for our Mary Joe. He has Mary Joe practicing six hours a day, and she doesn't seem to mind a bit."

Hmn, I'll bet she doesn't, thought Melissa, trying to catch her father's eye across the room. Aunt Sara's mouth grated on her nerves and she didn't care whether aunt Sara knew it or not. Jumping to her feet, she smiled sweetly and said, "Oh, I'm sorry Aunt Sara, but I simply must go over and give daddy a message— I forgot all about it until just now." Sara gave her niece a surprised look but smiled and told her to run along to her daddy.

On the other side of the drawing room. Clay and his brother Louie were in a deep discussion about politics and the price of cotton in North Carolina when Melissa came up and stood in front of them. She could feel aunt Sara's dark eyes boring into the middle of her back. Looking up at, uncle Louie remarked how pretty she looked in that shade of green, but then she always looked pretty to him anyway, he added. Please, with the compliment, Melissa grinned and said, "Uncle Louie, you do say the sweetest things to me."

Louis winked at Clay, "Well now," he replied, tongue in cheek, "isn't that what an uncle is for?"

Clay laughed and patted the seat of a chair beside him. "Come on sugar, sit down here, and listen to uncle Louie tell about his trip to North Carolina." Turning his head, he and Louie continued their talk. Melissa excused herself and walked over to the other side of the drawing room to where her mother, aunt, and the girls were seated. As she approached them she heard Mary Joe say, "Oh yes, aunt Luella, I really do enjoy playing the piano, that is, if you could call it playing—I'm afraid I haven't reached my goal as yet."

Oh! Not again! groaned Melissa, coming closer. Luella was staring deeply into Mary Joe's blue eyes, "My dear," she said, "your mother tells me you have an excellent piano teacher—a Mr. Devon?" she puckered her handsome forehead. "Now, I wonder if by any chance he's related to the Savannah Devons? They were certainly a musical family—quite accomplished, as I recall."

Sara appraised Melissa from head to foot as she came to a stop in front of them. She remarked slyly, "Well, I see you have delivered your message." Her tone said something else. Melissa murmured yes and sat down on the sofa beside Mary Joe. Patting Melissa's hand, Mary Joe said she was wondering when she was going to join them. Turning to Luella, she answered her question. "I couldn't say for sure, Aunt Luella. Hugh doesn't talk much about his family, although he mentioned something about Savannah." Mary Joe's angelic face was all smiles, talking about her favorite subject.

Nodding her head with a smile, Luella glanced at the Dresden mantle clock, "I see it's almost dinnertime," she said, "come on outside everybody."

They all stood up and followed Luella's graceful figure out the French door and down a small flight of steps onto the side lawn. The towering mansion cast a cool shadow across the green grass against the scorching hot sun. A small wooded area, densely populated with rich dark pine trees and thick brush, bordered one side of the verdant lawn. Luella called the place 'confederate haven' explaining that it once served as a hide-out for a group of war-weary confederate soldiers, when the Yankees pounced on Highacres. Over near the bushes there stood a large oval table resplendent with a white-damask tablecloth, gleaming silverware and a bowl of sweet-scented wild-roses and daisies in the center. A sparkling white-marble fountain nearby, gurgled and sprayed foamy water on chaste cherub faces gazing unseeingly into the water.

Sara beamed at the well-laid dinner table. "Luella Hampton, you certainly know how to arrange things! This is absolutely perfect! My goodness, I wish I had your 'know how' and thoughtfulness." Sarah's thick mouth stretched from ear to ear, "Mary Joe," she went on, "Take note, you can learn a lot from your Aunt Luella, you too, Linda May." She gave her daughter an amused glance. "But where would you practice the art of perfect entertaining in smelly hospital rooms?"

Linda May did not answer her mother. Instead, she took hold of Melissa's arm and asked how her charity work was coming along. Melissa replied that things were progressing nicely and that the finances were better now than ever.

"How nice!" smiled Linda May, "believe me, Melissa, charity is a vital part of our society." A far away expression came over her plain colorless features, and she added rather hesitantly, "I suppose that's why I want to go into medicine, one can give so much in that profession."

Melissa turned and gazed at her cousin's dumpy profile. "But aren't you afraid of being ridiculed?" she mildly asked as they sat down together at the dinner table. Linda May shrugged and looked away. Sara, already seated at the center of the table, reached out and plucked a daisy from the floral centerpiece and stuck it in her hair. "There now, I feel just like the kiss of spring," she playfully remarked. Mary Joe sat down beside her mother, a small smile moving her lovely mouth. Sometimes it was embarrassing listening to her mother's silly remarks, but one had to go along with her. It was the only way.

Clay grinned down the table at Sara, "May you always feel spring-like Sara, then you will never grow old... they say one is as old as one feels," he said, looking her straight in the eye.

"Then I am all of sixteen," returned Sara, laughing deep in her throat, "and I'm going to stay that way for the rest of my life!" The group laughed and joked their way through each course brought out of the house. Despite the mean temperature, Luella clung rigorously to her routine menu of roast beef, vegetables, potatoes, and corn bread topped off with a rich heavy dessert. The only concession she made was the two tall pitchers of iced lemonade, one on either end of the table. Congenial conversation drifted back and forth across the table, with an occasional throaty remarked from Sara about the peanut industry, then after a while, a cool breeze sprung up from out of nowhere, sweeping the feathery willow trees that stood near the fountain. Uncle Louie spoke with a sigh of relief. "Now, that sure feels good, doesn't it? Looks like we are in for some rain and I say, it's about time, my peanut crops are as dry as the Sahara desert." He turned to Clay and started expounding on the peanut market.

Sara frowned down the table at him. "Honestly, Louie," she complained in her frog-like tone, "it's a wonder to me you just don't turn into a peanut," turning away, she addressed the others, "that's all that man talks about at home... peanuts, peanuts, peanuts! I'm getting so I can't look one in the face." Sara's thick-set features tuned very sour. She pushed the luscious strawberry shortcake around on her cut-glass plate, as though it were to blame. Used to Sara's blatant outbursts about Louie's peanut farming, the family paid her no attention. Luella tactfully changed the subject. She asked, "Sara, would you care to go with me on a shopping trip to Augusta, Georgia sometime next week?"

Sara immediately brightened up. "I most certainly would, Luella," was her pleased reply. "I haven't been in Augusta in years, not since I was in the theater up north. How well I remember our troupe playing there; you wouldn't believe the generous reception we received—they really like us and they..."

"Yes, dear, I know," interrupted Luella hurriedly. The less said about Sara's stage career, the better. Taking another small helping of dessert, she went on, "Well then, Sara, it's a date. We can take an early train and be home again about seven in the evening." Melissa listened uninterestedly. Leave it to her beautiful mother to smooth things over. She knew she had invited aunt Sara on the spur of the moment. Her mother had once remarked that even though aunt Sara was a little rough around the edges, she had her good points, and one should help her develop them. Melissa wasn't sure of aunt Sara's good points—in her eyes, she was nothing but a coarse, ill-bred individual, but then weren't all northerners the same? Seated on Melissa's left at the table, Mary Joe was rattling on about her precious Mr. Devon, and on her right sat Linda May carefully explaining to her that the best medical schools were located up north and that she was eager to find out all about them. The two-way conversation was wearing her out.

The breeze was growing stronger now, and the sky suddenly overcast, hung heavy with rain. Melissa's hazel eyes moved slowly upward to a window on the third floor of the house. So far, Aunt Sara had kept still about Angela, and Melissa wondered why? She usually asked about her the minute she put her foot inside the house, and whether it was concern, or just her cat-like curiosity that prompted her, was hard to figure out.

Sara's deep voice boomed across the table, "What are you daydreaming about, Melly? A gentleman friend, perhaps?" Placing her fat elbows on the table, Sara cupped her cheeks in her hands and began dreamily, "Now, when I was an actress up north," Dear Me! Not again! Moaned Luella silently! Sara's voice softened a notch or two as she went on. "I had plenty of gentlemen friends waiting for me at the stage door—but I took none of them seriously, not until I met your handsome Uncle Louie! He literally swept me off my feet!"

Nobody said anything, least of all uncle Louie, who was busy talking to Clay. Suddenly, a clap of thunder shattered the silence, and dark clouds overhead burst in a terrific downpour.

Laughing and shouting to one another, the party scurried across the lawn and into the house, dripping wet. Luella rushed them into the parlor and turned on the gas heater in the fireplace for them to dry off. "Well," she laughed, "at least the weather was kind enough to let us finish our dessert." Fine beads of moisture trickled down her smooth forehead into her eyes. Dabbing her eyes with a handkerchief, she quietly asked if anyone would care for a cup of tea? They declined.

Louie spoke, "Luella," he remarked, his blue eyes twinkling, "I swear, if you were caught in the middle of an earthquake or some other disaster, you would stand your ground unperturbed as Venus de Milo."

Luella smiled and shook her head. "No, I don't think so, Louie. I'd probably be just as panicky as the next one."

Clay stood with his back toward the fire. "Luella dear," he said softly. "I'm afraid that's a matter of opinion. I don't believe I have ever seen you lose control, no matter what the situation." He gazed at her tenderly.

Teeming rain beat against the tall window panes and the lightening cutting across the sky, was soon fallowed by an earsplitting crash of thunder—it was a violent storm.

"My goodness!" cried Aunt Sara, "this is bad!" Turning to her husband, she moaned. "Louie, I hope to heaven we will make it home safely! You know thunder storms make me nervous as a cat! I'm deathly afraid of being hit by lightning!"

Louie came to her and laid his hand on her shoulder. "Now Sara," he soothed, "you now perfectly well, you're not going to be hit by lightning. The storm will abate in a few moments and we will be on our merry way, so stop worrying." Chucking her under her fat chin, he went back and sat down.

Sara gave Louie a dark look. "Hump!" *A lot you care! You care more for your old peanuts than you do me, anyway!* Louie laughed and turned away. Melissa gave her aunt a disgusted look, *What a fool of a woman! It's a wonder Uncle Louie hadn't divorced her years ago.*

Trying to clear the air, Luella asked Mary Joe to play the piano for them. Sara immediately brightened up. "Oh! Please do, dear," she urged, giving Mary Joe a loud kiss on the cheek. Turning to Luella and Clay. She loudly bragged, "My Mary Joe plays the piano beautifully! I just love listening to her." Luella nodded and smiled. Then led Mary Joe across the parlor to the white grand piano sitting in an alcove. "Here's some classic numbers, my dear," she said, arranging the music sheets on the rack. "Now just go ahead and play, and I'll join the others over there and enjoy it."

Mary Joe spun the piano stool around to her liking and carefully seated herself, her small hands resting in her lap. She frowned at the sheet of music on the rack. Alright. She could read music, but heavens! Not Mozart! Feeling very uncomfortable and foolish, Mary Joe realized she had better play something or other, so she started playing *Chop-Sticks* and got all the way through the piece without making a mistake. When she finished, she thought she heard snickers from across the room, and she knew it came from Melissa.

Rising sedately from the piano stool, she straitened her blue-voile dress, and walked across the room to the others. They politely clapped their hands and smiled as she approached the sofa. Sara called out to her, "Mary Joe, my pet! That was simply Marvelous! I must say that your handsome music teacher, Mr. Devon, is doing a fine job teaching you to play so well! Come on dear, squeeze in here beside Melissa and me. There's plenty of room on the sofa."

Melissa gazed at her cousin's exquisite profile. Now, if she could play the piano as well as she looked, Mozart and the rest of them would have to move over! But Mary Joe Hampton was not a pianist and never would be! My God! She mused. Even I can play silly old '*Chop-Sticks*', and I've never had a music lesson in my life!

Linda May, sitting on Melissa's left, stared hard into her cousin's face. "Melly," she remarked, "you look rather glum. Aren't you feeling well?"

Melissa turned around. "Linda May," she replied loftily, "of course I'm feeling well. Why did you ask me that?"

"Just wondering," smiled Linda May.

"See!" sputtered Sara.do "There she goes again! Pay her no mind, Melly, it's just doctor talk coming out of her mouth."

Linda May gave her mother a sad far-away look, then turned and spoke to her Aunt Luella. The afternoon wore on, and it finally stopped raining. Sara and her two daughters put on their hats, ready to leave. On the other side of the parlor, Clay and Louie were discussing the upcoming Mayoral election that was to take place in Batesburg, the following week.

"Now, Clay." Argued Louie, rolling his protruding eyes, "that Marks guy is nothing but a phony. No guts at all! We don't need that sort running our town!"

Clay smiled and shook his head. "Now, Louis," he replied calmly, "you know as well as I do, that the best man is going to win, and we will simply have to go along with it."

Sara stood in the middle of the floor, glaring at her husband. "Well," she snapped with a toss of her head. "Are we going home now or not? Or are we going to wait until it rains pitchforks again? Really!"

"I'm coming, I'm coming," Louie returned amicably. Rising slowly from his chair, he rubbed his knees, adding, "This danged weather always gets into these old bones of mine!"

Sara started tapping her foot on the floor, scowling at Louie. "Never mind your silly old bones!" She sniffed, "just move them, that's all!"

Luella began to get quite nervous. She had witnessed Sara's pitiable lack of control before—the woman was sadly in need of finesse—probably due to her improper upbringing, thought Luella, leading her visitors to the front door. Saying goodbye, with hugs and kisses, Louie, Sara, Mary Joe, and Linda May moved carefully down the slippery front steps and got into their carriage, Luella, and Clay stood waving on the front porch, then went inside. Melissa was in the foyer idly flipping through the pages of a book. Luella gave her a stern look. "Melissa," she said, "don't you think you were rather rude not saying goodbye to your Aunt Sara and the girls?"

"I said goodbye to Uncle Louie, didn't I?" she replied absently.

Clay raised his eyebrows at his daughter. "Don't be rude to your aunt and cousins, Melly. I'm sure it won't get you anywhere."

"Daddy," replied Melissa patiently, "you know I have no use for Aunt Sara. She's always showing off about something, and more than that, she says nasty things to me!"

Raising her eyebrows, Luella looked at Clay and he shrugged as though to say, *that's our daughter.* "Melissa," Luella began coolly, "I didn't hear Sara say anything mean to you. I'm afraid your imagination runs away with your at times. Now, we'll hear no more of it!" Her head held high, Luella turned and moved gracefully into the parlor.

Melissa gazed at her father, "Daddy," she began quietly, "I'm sorry, but honestly, I just can't abide Aunt Sara, and I think you know it. Furthermore, I'm sure Mary Joe and Linda May will be just as unbearable when they grow older."

Clay stared soberly in his lovely daughter's face, and sighed, *Well, she will never be another Luella, no indeed. Not Melissa!* A painful expression on his rugged face, his thoughts traveled upstairs to his other daughter, Angela; in appearance, she was truly Luella. Same large green eyes, same even temperament, that is, until her poor troubled mind took over. At times, Angela would be lucid as the next one, then without warning, she would start to moan and pace back and forth across her bedroom floor, muttering all kinds of gibberish.

"Melissa," replied Clay sadly, "you must control your attitude towards people. As you travel through life, my dear, you will bump into people, this one and that one, who will rub you the wrong way; and you will learn to grin and bear it. It happens to all of us, you know."

Melissa stood staring down at the highly polished foyer floor. Clay's calm, even tone touched her deeply, as it always did. She looked up at his tall slender figure, and gray-streaked Auburn hair, realizing how much she loved him.

"I love you, Daddy," she murmured, "and I promise to not let things bother me so much."

Clay walked over to her. "I know you will, Lissie."

Melissa strolled into the parlor and dropped down in an easy chair beside her mother.

"Melissa," said Luella, a concerned expression on her face. "I think we had better go up and check on Angela. I'm afraid that awful storm has upset her."

Melissa nodded, and they walked into the foyer. As they climbed the stairs, Luella remarked that she thought it was fine of Mary Joe, entering the Medical field, and that she would be a dedicated doctor. Melissa frowned and said nothing. When they reached Angela's room on the third floor, the door suddenly burst open, and Angela, her eyes rolling wildly, stood rigid in the doorway. Luella and Melissa gently led her inside to her bed.

"Angela, my darling," whispered Luella, "please lie down on the bed for a while. Melissa and mother are with you. There is nothing to be afraid of now."

Whimpering with fright, Angela stared awhile at her mother, then laid down on the bed, closing her eyes. A door opened across the room, and Mrs. Nora Bennet, Angela's nurse, entered the room. "She'll be alright Mrs. Hampton," she smiled. "The storm terrified her, as they always do. I gave her a sedative a few moments ago."

Stroking Angela's forehead, Melissa started humming a tune from their childhood, as Mrs. Bennet approached the bed and took hold of the girl's thin wrist, checking her pulse. Smiling softly, she turned to Luella saying, "Angela will probably sleep until morning, she will be fine, I promise." Luella sighed, and tenderly kissed Angela's cheek.

When Luella and Melissa came downstairs, they went into the parlor again and settled down in their easy chairs. Bright sunlight streamed through the rich Austrian lace curtains on the windows, and Luella's antique grandfather clock, the one she brought from Savannah, struck five. Melissa gazed at the far-away expression on her attractive mother's face - Luella was "still upstairs" with Angela, and it was no wonder! Melissa looked away. Sad thoughts crowding her mind; she loved her sister completely, desperately! When they were growing up together, she would hold Angela close, telling her not to ever be afraid, for no matter what, her sister would always protect her, and keep nasty people from hurting her—such as Aunt Sara!

Melissa frowned and slid down in her chair. Daddy adored Angela too, he would often stand at the foot of the stairs gazing upward, with a deep hurt look in his soft-gray eyes.

Luella spoke, "Melissa, why don't you sit up straight? I can almost see your stockings."

Melissa rose and, moving slowly across the room to the wide bay windows, she drew the blinds all the way down to the sill. Luella smiled and asked, "Are you afraid of that lovely sunshine, Melissa?"

"No," replied Melissa, returning to her easy chair, "I felt a little warm, that's all."

"I see," said Luella, quietly. She was silent a while, then went on, "Don't you think Angela looked paler than usual, Melissa? I hope and pray she is not coming down with anything!"

Melissa gazed up at the cherubs floating around on the parlor ceiling - it took her back to her childhood, and how she would dash in here whenever she was troubled about something, and stare up at them for a long time. She turned to Luella. "Mother, that awful storm terrified our poor Angela so much that her own poor little world seemed to crash around her. She's on my mind constantly and sometimes I can hardly bear it! It would kill me if anything happened to her!"

Luella sat gazing at her lovely youngest daughter; she thanked fate, or whatever it was, that she was born strong and healthy. And how lovely she is! Her chestnut hair is like tarnished copper, and with her large hazel eyes, and trim figure, she will surely be a prize for some youn man, that is, if she learns to control her obstinate, independent nature.

At dinner that evening, Clay addressed his wife seated at the head of the long dining room table. A crystal chandelier spread a comforting light on the sparkling silverware, stoneware china, and the cut-glass bowl of pink roses in the center of the table. Luella looked up with a smile. "Yes Clay, what is it?"

Laying down his knife and fork, he asked her if Louie or Sara had mentioned anything about the old Jefferson place.

"No Clay, they didn't," replied Luella, buttering a hot roll, "you know, I've been wondering if those Northerners who bought it had settled there yet." She thought awhile, "My goodness! I've been told that the Jefferson family has owned that plantation since the eighteenth century."

"Hmn, that so?" grunted Clay, helping himself to another slice of delicious baked ham.

Melissa listened quietly. She had heard Aunt Sara often enough say how perfectly lovely it was going to be having Northerners for a neighbor and that she could hardly wait to meet them. Melissa wanted to discuss Angela, not a pack of strangers! Frowning irritably, she took another helping of candied yams, and concentrated on her plate.

Luella noticed how quickly Melissa was eating her foodtable and knew something was bothering her. Clay noticed it also, "Lissy," he grinned, "you'll choke eating so fast."

Melissa kept on eating, and after a while she asked to be excused, saying she had to review the charity meeting report. "Alright, Melissa," sighed Luella, "you may be excused." Clay sighed and shook his head.

Hurrying upstairs to her bedroom, Melissa flung herself on her bed, her head was full of the awful embarrassment she had suffered that afternoon at the charity club. Nobody seemed to understand how she felt, neither her mother nor her daddy -

didn't he laugh at her? Well! She'd never go through that again! Furthermore, how could she ever forget the surprised expression on that man's face when she stumbled down those danged steps into his arms! Rolling over, Melissa buried her face in the bed pillow. But, I wonder she he is and where did he come from? She wondered and wondered, then angry with herself, she muttered, "Well, who cares anyway?" Jumping off the bed, Melissa walked over to her dressing table, and stared at herself in the mirror. I wish I was more like my mother," she thought. She knows how to handle anything.

$\maltese$ 2 $\maltese$

T HE J EFFERSON HOUSE adjoining Louie and Sara Hampton's property was now occupied; it had come alive again, with its wide green lawn, lush rose bushes, and general air of comfort.

George Belden, tall, blond, and serious, stood on the wide pillared porch contemplating his property. Perhaps he would raise a few acres of cotton - not too much, just enough to help pay expenses. His father died two years before, leaving him and his twin brother, John, amply provided for. So, while on a trip to Batesburg, South Carolina, George fell in love with the old Jefferson plantation, and bought it; for he truly loved the South - the beautiful blue mountains, the verdant meadows, and most of all, the delightful southern hospitality. Though reared up North in Chicago, his heart and soul were in the South. Was it because his great grandfather whom he was named for, was born in the South (Georgia, in fact), and had bravely fought in the Civil War? George smile, and walked into his house. It was cool and peaceful in the dim foyer, and a delicious aroma of baked ham permeated the hallway.

Strolling into his spacious old-fashioned parlor, George sat down in an easy chair, relaxed and happy, thinking how good it made him feel to own a beautiful place like this! He wondered if these people would really accept him; he'd heard somewhere that the South was still fighting the Civil War, and that all the Northerners were just plain dirt! With a smile, he recalled how his brother John scoffed at his plan - *How in the world could he run a large plantation?* He asked. *Especially amongst a bunch of rebels!* He told George he was a complete idiot for living in the South.

The front doorbell startled him, and he heard Delila Jones, his colored housekeeper, hurrying down the hall to answer it. Perhaps it was the real estate agent calling to see if all was well. Delila's rollicking laughter filled the foyer, and a feminine voice joined in.

"Honey," chuckled Delila, "Mr. George is in the parlor. Just go right in."

Sara Hampton, a broad smile on her face, breezed into the parlor and held out her hand to George. "Mr. Belden," she gushed, "I'm your next-door neighbor, Sara Hampton. My husband, Louis and I wish to welcome you to Batesburg. Now, please let us know if we can help you in any way."

Smiling broadly, Sara plumped down in an easy chair. "Louis and I have two lovely daughters," she went on, "Mary Joe is our eldest daughter, and Linda May; I call Linda May our *doctor daughter*, for she is studying medicine and I don't know whether I like it or not."

George stood up. "Well! How very nice. This is very friendly of you, Mrs. Hampton. I really don't know what to say, other than thank you," he said, thankful a Southerner accepted him.

"Oh, by the way, Mr. Belden, do you happen to come from Chicago?" asked Sara, smiling up in his face.

"True enough," grinned George.

"Oh! For goodness' sake!" exclaimed Sara. "I'm from Chicago too. I used to be on the stage up north, you know, but I married a Southerner, and here I am!" Sara grinned and patted the curly fringe of hair on her forehead.

"Well, Mr. Belden," she cooed, "I'm sure I've taken up enough of our time. And as I said before, please let us know if you should need anything at anytime, ta ta!" Sara tuned and hurried out of the room, quite impressed with the very handsome Mr. Belden. What a fine catch he'd be for her Linda May! She thought as she opened the front door and trotted down the steps to her carriage.

George sat in his chair, an amused smile on his face. The woman is pushy and 'put-on', he thought, stretching his long arms over his head, but friendly enough, I guess.

Glancing at the clock, he decided to drive into town and talk to a landscape man about a few changes he wanted on his property. The grand old Jefferson plantation was quite close to his heart. Its refined atmosphere, lofty ceilings and spacious rooms did a lot for his soul. In the early mornings, George would often stroll through the mansion, room by room, enjoying a solitude he had never known before.

Yes! He would take good care of the fine old place, as long as he lived, and brother John could scoff his head off!

Arriving in town that afternoon, George took care of the business at hand, then strolled idly down the main thoroughfare, gazing into the interesting shop windows. He admired attractive little Batesburg, with its tall elm tres casting shadows on the wrought-iron benches placed conveniently here and there along the wooden walks; and the horse-drawn carriages clip-clopping down the cobblestone streets, bespoke Southern charm. Coming to one of the town's oldest restaurants, George hesitated, then walked inside, and he sat at a table near the window.

The large room was airy, having fern plants in brass jardinières placed tastefully around the floor and snowy damask tablecloths on small round tables stood out like graceful magnolia blossoms.

George sighed, and after giving his order to a waiter, he settled back in his chair and lit a cigarette. Sitting at a table in the center of the room, Melissa Hampton, and her Charity Club friend, Janet Lane, were eye to eye across the table, in deep conversation. Suddenly, Melissa stopped talking and stared hard in George's direction.

"Janet," she cried excitedly, "there's that man I fell on at the charity meeting last month! I know it's him! Look!"

Janet turned and gazed across the room at George. "Gosh! Mel, I don't know. He looks familiar... a little."

"Oh! Of course it's him!" returned Melissa irritably. "I never was so embarrassed in all my life when I tripped down those stupid steps, right into his arms. You remember that, don't you?"

Janet nodded yes. "But Mel," she advised slowly, "I think you should forget it. It was just an accident."

"Oh, yes?" cried Melisa, her voice rising sharply, "if it happened to you, Janet Lane, I'd never hear the end of it! And now you sit there shaking your head at me, as though I were a five-year-old!"

By this time, heads were turning in the restaurant. George looked curiously across the room at the two girls, wondering what they were arguing about. Watching them walk toward the entrance, on their way out, he had an idea he had seen the petite one before; and it suddenly came to him. He started to laugh, recalling how very flustered that delightful young lady was that day at the Charity Club, as she dashed out the front door.

❦   3   ❦

SARA AND LOUIS HAMPTON sat relaxed on a swinging hammock on their wide stone veranda. A warm October sun gently kissed the tall oak trees, ablaze with color, the freshness of fall permeated the surroundings.

Smiling contentedly, Sara let out a deep sigh, and turning to Louis, she coyly suggested giving a masquerade ball on the thirty-first. "Louie!" she added excitedly. "I think it's a marvelous idea, don't you?" Eyeing Louie expectantly, she continued, "We could invite Mr. Belden, our brand new neighbor, and get better acquainted. He is such a nice person, you know, intelligent, well educated and quite charming. I'm sure our Linda May would be delighted to meet him."

Louie turned and stared at his wife. "Now, just a minute there, just a minute. How do you know whether this Mr. Belden would care to attend our party? Northerners don't take much to us, you know."

"Well, pish-tosh!" snapped Sara, her dark eyes flashing. "Have you forgotten that I took you? And haven't I gone right along with your old corn-pone, and Confederate flag?"

Louie nodded. "Yes, my dear, indeed you have," he said. "And I'm real proud of you, too."

"Well, thank you for the compliment, sir!" frowned Sara, sitting back on the hammock. After a while, she spoke again, "The girls and I will start planning immediately. Our ball is going to be the finest in Batesburg! My goodness!" she sighed. "Just thinking of it takes me back to my theater days. I'll have to brush up one of my old routines and give a performance." Sara glanced at Louie. "I can still sing, whether you think so or not."

Louie opened a newspaper, saying nothing.

❦

The next day, Sara gushed to Mary Joe and Linda May, how lovely their masquerade ball would be. Nothing would be spared, she said. And of course, she would kindly ask those invited to wear a costume.

Mary Joe was delighted. "Oh, mother!" she cried. "I think it's a marvelous idea. I can hardly wait! You know what? I'll ask Hugh to play the piano for us."

Linda May listened quietly, not sure whether she liked it or not. His medical studies were piling up, and it would be awkward finding the time for a masquerade ball.

Sara gazed at her youngest daughter. "Well," she said, "you don't seem very interested in the ball. Got an operation scheduled for that night?" She added sarcastically.

Linda May sighed. "Mother," she started mildly, "you say the silliest things at times." Turning away, she walked calmly out of the parlor and down the dim hall to the kitchen. Her head ached, and she was tired, for she had stayed up till dawn poring over medical books. Furthermore, she needed a cup of coffee. Opening the kitchen door, she moved over to the sink and filled the teakettle with water, and set it on the range. Sitting down on a chair, she stared into space, thinking.

Linda May realized she was scoffed at for wanting to be a doctor, not only by her mother, but by Melissa as well; and Mary Joe, so taken with her piano teacher, probably didn't care one way or another, whether her sister became a doctor or a street cleaner! Linda May wondered what being in love was all about. Not that she was interested in the emotion, her only aim in life was to heal people and make them laugh.

Finishing her coffee, she strolled out the rear door onto the terrace and sat down on a rustic bench under an oak tree. It was cool and shady, high up in the green foliage. The sound of happy chirping birds made her smile.

Glancing idly across the hedge at the Jefferson place, she remembered her mother saying she would also invite the new owner, Mr. Belden, to the masquerade ball. Linda May shrugged and went back into the house. When she walked down the hall into the foyer, she noticed Mary Joe standing before the hall mirror, fluffing her honey-blonde hair. Smiling at her sister in the mirror, Mary Joe said, "I can't understand why you're not thrilled about the ball, Linda May. I can hardly wait to tell Hugh when he comes this evening. He's coming to help me with the classical numbers I keep stumbling over. Say! You look ready to drop! Didn't you get any sleep last night?"

"No, not much, I guess. I was studying."

Mary Joe started to laugh. "You're always studying, aren't you? Not for me, thank you, I'll take music. Well, good luck Dr. Hampton!"

Turning away from the mirror, she strolled into the parlor and sat down, waiting for Hugh.

Sara, coming slowly down the wide stairway, eyed the two of them. "Stay right there, Linda May!" she called out, "I want to talk to you." Taking Linda May's arm, she steered her into the library, and closed the door. Sitting down on a sofa in the warm glow of a hurricane lamp, Sara motioned Linda May to sit down beside her; a wide grin on her coarse face, she patted her daughter's hand and began.

"My dear," she said, "I want you to listen closely to what I have to say. Now, I want nothing more in this world than to see my girls happily married." Sara cleared her throat. "When I was your age, I was completely stage struck. It was my life, and I loved it! However, when your father appeared on the scene, I forgot all about acting and silly things like that. Now, what I'm leading up to is this. I wish you would give up this silly idea of becoming a doctor, and look for a nice young man to marry." She paused a moment, hoping what she had said to Linda May had sunk in. "Now, my dear," she continued sweetly, "about our ball, I'm sure it will be a great success. We'll all wear costumes, of course, so you had better start thinking of one for yourself."

Sara gave her daughter a sour glance. "And for heaven's sake, please stay away from a nurse's uniform! We don't need that!"

Linda May eyed her mother coldly. Sara wasn't Sara unless she ran someone's life. Well, she thought grimly, she'll never run mine. Rising from the sofa, she slowly crossed the room to the library doorway and turned around. "Mother," she said calmly, "I intend to control my own life and become a doctor, and whether you agree or not is immaterial to me. Furthermore, I doubt I'll ever marry. The thought does not interest me in the least. I guess that settles the issue, does it not?"

Sara glared across the room at Linda May. "Now let me tell you a thing or two, miss!" she cried. "If you keep on thinking that way all your life, you'll be strictly alone when you reach my age! And I hope your stinky old medicine bottles will keep you company!"

By this time, Linda May was half-way up the broad stairway. Her mother's sharp high-pitched voice echoed in the foyer.

4

MELISSA AND LUELLA sat in the Hampton parlor, sorting the morning mail. "Well, my goodness!" exclaimed Luella, raising her Savanna eyebrows, "Sara and Louie are giving a masquerade ball on the thirty-first, and we are all invited. Hmn!" She went on, "She asks us to wear costumes. I don't know about that."

Melissa took the invitation and read it. "Well, I think it's a great idea," she said, her lovely eyes sparkling. "Maybe I'll go as Cinderella."

"Yes," nodded Luella, "and you'll be a lovely one too. I must ask Sara if she needs my help."

"There is also a note in here," said Melissa. "I'll read it to you; Aunt Sara says *she inviting that Yankee who bought the old Jefferson place.* I don't think she should invite a perfect stranger to the ball, do you? And an old Yankee at that!"

"Now Melissa," returned Luella calmly, "is it not Aunt Sara's business whom she invites to the ball?"

"Hmp!" grunted Melissa. "I suppose so, but Mother, not a Yankee!"

"Never mind. Just go and see if you can find your father. I want to talk to him."

❧

The night of the ball, Melissa stood admiring herself before a pier mirror in her bedroom. Her rose-colored Cinderella costume brought out the copper glint in her thick auburn hair; and as she swung from side to side before the mirror, she fluffed the dainty chiffon folds of her costume, glowing with pleasure. Nodding in satisfaction, and feeling like Cinderella herself, she left her bedroom and descended the stairway with a strange excitement taking hold of her, which caused her heart to beat a lot faster than usual.

Luella, resplendent as *Mary Queen of Scots,* and Clay in a daring pirate costume stood awaiting in the foyer. "Melly honey," exclaimed Clay, moving toward her, "you all look sweet enough to kiss!" Grabbing hold of her, he kissed her soundly on the cheek.

Luella eyed her daughter from head to toe. "Yes indeed, my dear," she agreed. "I must say you look very nice as Cinderella. Well, let's go now. Sara will probably be waiting for us." They walked out of the front door and down the steps to their carriage.

Sara and Louis Hampton stood greeting arriving guests in the tall archway that divided their drawing room and foyer. The stately mansion hummed with happy laughter and music. The guests all wore masks and when Luella, Clay, and Melissa arrived, Sara gushed how marvelous they looked in costume. "Of course," she whispered. "I'm not supposed to recognize anyone under their masks. Just join the others in the drawing room. Mary Joe and Linda May are somewhere in there, but I'm not telling you what costumes they're wearing." She paused and looked toward the drawing room. "I'm so excited and I'm afraid I'll be too nervous to give a proper performance later on tonight."

Uncle Louie, arrayed in a bright red and green clown costume, stood shaking his head

The orchestra was playing a waltz as they strolled into the drawing room, and Luella and Clay immediately joined the dancers on the wide polished floor.

Melissa gazed idly around the room, wondering where Mary Joe and Linda May were. Perhaps the ball wouldn't be so much fun after all, thought Melissa, especially with everyone wearing masks.

Suddenly, her eye caught a tall, slim man wearing a blue-satin Prince Costume, crossing the room in her direction. Pausing before her with an elaborate bow, he asked politely, "Cinderella, may I have this waltz?"

Melissa nodded, and as they glided gracefully onto the floor, she started at his blue mask, wishing she could pull it off and see his face. After a while, the music stopped, and they found themselves surrounded by Kings, Queens, clowns, Pirates, and the like, talking and laughing with one another; the ornate drawing room glowed with warmth and fun.

The orchestra started playing another waltz tune, and once again Melissa and the tall stranger swung around the dance floor, as though they were dancing on air, until the music stopped. The Prince escorted Melissa back to the sofa and sat down beside her. "My goodness!" she laughed. "I do believe I'm out of breath. I don't know who you are, sir, but you sure are a fine dancer."

"And you also, little Cinderella," returned the Prince. "I thought I was holding a feather in my arms."

In no time at all, it was midnight. Aunt Sara, standing before the orchestra, called out in her shrill tone, "Ladies and gentlemen, please unmask and come onto the dance floor. This lovely orchestra is going to play one of my old numbers. As some of you know, I was once on the stage, and I loved it! So, with your kind indulgence, I will sing for you. Also, our Mary Joe's piano teacher, Mr. Hugh Devon, has kindly offered to play for us. Now, isn't that nice?"

Everybody removed their masks and quietly gathered on the dance floor to hear Aunt Sara sing. As Melissa and the tall stranger walked onto the floor, she quickly glanced up in his face and froze with embarrassment. He was the man she fell on at the Charity Club.

George Belden smiled down at her, saying, "Miss Cinderella, I do believe we have met before." Melissa blushed, not saying a word. "Oh, come now," whispered George playfully, "don't be shy."

"I'm not shy, Mr. So and So," returned Melissa flippantly, "I'm mortified, thinking how clumsy I was that day at the Charity Club. Anyway," she added, "I thank you kindly for saving my life!"

Grinning broadly, George introduced himself, saying it had been a distinct pleasure catching her in his arms. Melissa then introduced herself, and they joined the others on the floor. Luella and Clay, with Mary Joe and Linda May, stood in back of them, and the performance began.

Sara, not at all in voice, managed to struggle through her number; and the look on Uncle Louie's face told it all. Hugh Devon played the piano exquisitely; the applause he received reached the rafters. All in all, Sara's ball was a success, and saying goodnight to her guests later that evening, Sara smiled here and smiled there, immensely with herself, promising to give more balls in the future.

In the carriage on their way home, Clay turned and asked Melissa if she had enjoyed Aunt Sara's ball.

Mr. George Belden, deep in her mind, Melissa replied, "I sure did, daddy."

"I thought so," returned Clay, grinning. "Isn't that young fellow you danced with, Sara and Louie's new neighbor?"

"Yes, clay, he is," interjected Luella, "don't you remember Sara introducing us?" she went on, "His name is George Belden, his is an acceptable young man, as far as appearance goes, but he is a Northerner."

"Well, mother, what's the difference?" frowned Melissa.

"There's a lot of difference, young lady," responded Luella loftily. "We Southerners do not mix with Northerners. You should know that, Melissa."

Melissa stayed quiet for the rest of the journey home. She liked George Belden more than she cared to admit, in fact, she liked him a lot more than other young men she knew in Batesburg. George Belden impressed her deeply, and she wanted to see him again, Northerner or not.

❧

The day after the ball, George sat at his desk in the library checking household expenses. Though not in need of money, he kept a keen eye on his budget, and having found the home he longed for int he gentle south, he was determined to apply himself wholeheartedly to the lovely estate.

Clasping his hands behind his head, he recalled the enjoyable Halloween ball the night before. His talkative neighbor outdid herself as hostess; very jolly woman, he mused. George smiled again. The other Hampton family also amused him, pure

Southern grace there, especially Miss Melissa. A soft expression crossed George's face. He would see that lovely young lady again, or his name wasn't George Belden.

Delila entered the library, waving a yellow envelope. "Mr. Belden," she said, "a boy just delivered this here telegram for you." She put it on his desk and left the room. George opened it and read, "Hi there, brother. I'll arrive on November third." He grinned and shook his head. Leave it to an impulsive John! Nice surprise, thought George as he pushed back in his chair and left the room.

THE COMPANION

❧ I ☙

ENGLAND, 1860

✦

There was no way of knowing yet whether I would regret accepting the position of companion at Longdon Hall. I stood waiting on the shabby station platform, shivering in the cold. The raw November weather penetrated my bones. I wondered what I would do if nobody came for me. I would never be able to find my own way to Longdon Hall. A half-hour passed, then another, and still no sign of a carriage on the dim road.

Deciding I must do something, I picked up my heavy carpetbag and entered the station house, and walked over to the ticket window. An oil lamp flickering feebly on the other side of the counter revealed a man's sour-looking face bent over some papers. I asked him if he knew whether or not Longdon Hall was sending a carriage for me. He stared up at me. "Longdon Hall?" he queried. His eyebrows came together in a straight black line, as though he was trying to figure it out. He gave me a curious smile, wondering why I wanted to go there. "Ye never can tell about them there folks up at the hall," he watched my face and then asked, "Are ye going to work at the Hall?" I nodded. The ticket agent bundled up his papers and shoved them in a drawer. I could tell he was pondering something before going on with what he had to say. Giving me a sympathetic look he said, "Don't ye worry miss, I'm sure a carriage will come along soon." Turning his back, he left me to think it over. I walked outside into the purple-black silence. There were no bird calls. Not even a whisper of wind stirred the branches of the tall elm tree under which I stood.

Having advertised the previous week for a position of companion, I immediately received a beautifully hand-written reply and, after returning the required references, I was accepted and instructed to come to Longdon Hall at my earliest convenience. I was now in a remote part of England, totally unfamiliar to me. For having been born in southern England, I had never traveled more than ten miles from my home in all my life. My mother died when I was born and having no sisters or brothers, but a very selfish stepmother who treated me badly, I soon stuck out for myself.

The cold night air crawled up and down my spine. I shivered miserably as I drew my woolen shawl more tightly around my thin body. The station-master had long since gone home to his cottage across the way; I had watched his lantern go out of sight, feeling very uneasy. Two hours had passed since I stepped off the train and it looked as though I would have to spend the long dreary night on the station platform. As this unwelcome thought bounced around in my mind, I heard a carriage come towards me and stop. A lantern was shoved in my face and a rough voice asked, "Are ye, Jennifer Marks?" The lantern reflected the coarse wrinkled face of a man about sixty years old. A fringe of untidy gray-black hair fell in his eyes, giving him a clownish look. Leaning down, the man stared in my face and his tobacco breath almost gagged me. Sprier than any cricket I ever saw, he jumped down from the carriage and flung my carpetbag on the seat, telling me to get in. The old man turned the carriage around and, shouting at the horses, took off at a fast clip down the road.

I thought we would never reach Longdon Hall. We rode over wide heaths and down deep ravines past shadowy wooded areas and up the other side onto other heaths until the road branched sharply around a group of giant oak trees. My driver told me we were now on Longdon property with two more miles to go. We rode on and on across a wide moor, then, turning to the left, rode under a canopy of tall dark elms for about half a mile. Rounding a sharp curve in the driveway, we finally came to a stop in front of Longdon Hall. I got out of the carriage and stood looking up at the moonlit spires and high tower on the roof. I was carried away in imagination to another time and place. It seemed strangely familiar, yet unreal.

"Ye'd better look sharp, miss," grumbled the driver. "Lord John, he don't like to be kept waiting. Well, I thought, he didn't mind keeping me waiting, did he? Feeling a little miffed, I watched the old man drag my carpet bag off the carriage seat and trudge up the wide stone steps, and I followed him. He banged the heavy iron knocker several times before the high arched door finally swung open. A pale young face peered at us. "Well? Nellie? Stand aside! Stand aside!" exclaimed the old man. The girl opened the door wider, and I found myself standing in a large rotunda. A huge glass dome towered high over my head. I had never seen anything like it in my life! There was a winding staircase on the left side of the rotunda leading up to circular galleries on the second, third, and fourth floors of the house, each having rooms opening off of them. Brilliant moonlight slanted through the great glass dome, lighting up the rotunda like day. I later learned that the dome was exactly one hundred feet from its center to the center of the rotunda floor. I was also informed that Lord Longdon had remodeled the entrance and upper floors of the house after St. Paul's Cathedral in London.

As I stood under that massive dome on my first night at Longdon Hall, I felt as if I had suddenly been transported to some far-off planet where only special people resided and I, a complete stranger, might at any moment be told to leave.

I had not long to wait for my new employer. He appeared suddenly out of nowhere, greeting me in a deep compelling voice. He asked me if I was Miss Jennifer Marks? I found myself gazing up at a very tall man whose deep-set eyes appraised me from head to toe. His pale, clear-cut, handsome face frightened me and attracted me. I answered quietly that I was Jennifer Marks. Mr. Longdon. I found out later that he preferred the simpler title, gave me a closer look and idly remarked, "Young woman, you look like you have been dipped in ice! Did you wait a long time for my carriage?" His eyes mocked me. And before I had a chance to say anything, he grabbed hold of my arm with his strong fingers and steered me into a spacious drawing-room. Crystal chandeliers hung like sparkling jewels from the high white ceiling. There was luxury everywhere in this stunning room, from the priceless oil paintings on the walls to the soft green carpeting underfoot.

Mr. Longdon led me over to a long green velvet sofa in front of a white marble fireplace and told me to sit down. "I'll ring for tea," he said, moving gracefully across the wide room to a bell cord. Having very little flesh on my small, angular body, I was chilled to the bone after my long wait at the station, and a hot cup of tea sounded good to me. I was feeling awkward in the luxurious room in my plain brown-serge dress and woolen shawl and bonnet. I have never been considered pretty with my broad face and flat smile, yet I had a mass of thick auburn hair which I wore parted down the middle and coiled low on the back of my neck. My oversized hazel eyes were inherited from my mother, and I was pleased with them but, I had no illusions as to my looks.

A short stocky woman about fifty years old entered the drawing-room carrying a tray of tea and cakes. She gave me a curious look as she hurriedly set the tray down on the table and left the room.

"I see Mrs. Childs is in a hurry again," laughed my new employer. Pouring some tea in a delicate china teacup and handing it to me. "Good woman though, she has been with us over twenty years," he said. Mr. Longdon's smile was fascinating. Feeling much warmer and more at ease, I leaned back on the sofa, my eyes on his face, waiting for him to speak. But instead, he got up and started pacing the floor, his hands behind his back. Ten minutes passed, and I wondered if he had forgotten me, then, coming to a halt in front of me, he stared down at me in a strange way and said, "Miss Marks, I sincerely hope you will like working at Longdon hall." I smiled up at him, saying only a fool would complain. Holding my eye, he started explaining my duties. He told me I would be his mother's companion, and that she has a failing heart which often kept her confined to her bed, though most of the time she was up and around. He stopped speaking, then went on, "I shall expect you to see to things up there." I wondered why he was picking his words so carefully. "My mother needs company. I'm too busy to spend much time with her," he said bluntly. His cold manner concerning his mother shocked me.

I came to my feet, not saying anything, and watched him cross the room and pull the bell cord. The housekeeper soon appeared in the drawing-room, and Mr. Longdon waved in my direction and said, "Mrs. Childs, this is my mother's new companion, Miss Jennifer Marks. Will you please show her up to her quarters on the fourth floor?" Bidding me a crisp goodnight, he brushed past the woman into the foyer and his footsteps loud and clear faded away in the distance.

Mrs. Childs gave me a friendly smile, telling me to follow her out into the foyer, then lighting a tall candle, beckoned me up the winding stairway, my carpet bag held firmly in her hand. We climbed up, up and around, coming at last onto the fourth-floor gallery. The candle held high over her gray head. Mrs. Childs led me midway around the gallery to an oak doorway. She opened the door, and we went inside. She set the brass candlestick down on a marble-topped table in the center of the room, then told me in a soft, pleasant voice that she had been a housekeeper at Longdon Hall for many years. "Ah yes," she said, "and a grand house it is too, only for her in there," she whispered, jerking her head towards a doorway opening off the room we were in. I didn't like the way she said, "*her in there*". It seemed to spell trouble.

Mrs. Childs laughed and patted my shoulder. She went on telling me who else lived at Longdon Hall besides Mr. Longdon and his mother. There was Mr. Longdon's younger brother Robin, there was their 80-year-old uncle Thorne Longdon. "And he's a tiresome handful at times," she added. "Lady Longdon takes her meals in her room," said Mrs. Childs, "and so will you, my dear. Breakfast is at eight and lunch is at twelve-thirty, and dinner is at six p.m., you may have the afternoon tea if you wish." She smiled and showed me a speaking tube on the wall near the gallery doorway. "This tube leads down to the kitchen and to my bedroom. Should you ever need anything, just speak loudly into the mouthpiece and I'll come right away."

Walking over top the window, Mrs. Childs closed the red-velvet drapes then lighted a rose-colored lamp on a small round table in the area, then went over and poked the live coals in the fireplace. Her beaming, friendly face warmed me more than the heat from the grate. I liked her. "Well, I'll be leaving you now. I hope you'll be warm and comfortable. There's one thing, sure," she said, pointing to a tall bookcase over in the corner of the room, "you will find plenty of books to read over there. Mr. Longdon believes everybody should read good books, he sees that they are in every room in the Hall."

I mumble my thanks, then said, "By the way, Mrs. Childs, should I introduce myself to Lady Longdon tonight?" It was already past nine o'clock; Mrs. Childs replied with a frown. "I would wait until tomorrow if I were you, Miss Marks, Lady Longdon does not like her sleep disturbed. We are quite watchful of that."

I said, "Yes, I understand. I'm afraid I'm much too tired tonight to make an impression." Nodding her head, Mrs. Childs kindly bid me goodnight and left the room. I took off my bonnet and shawl and sat down in a comfortable armchair by the warm fireplace. I leaned back with my eyes closed, exhausted. I began to wonder if I would be contented at Longdon Hall and why Mr. Longdon made me feel uneasy. Was it because of the far-away look in his dark eyes and his abrupt goodnight to me as he left the drawing-room? What I needed was a good night's sleep. Opening my eyes, I gazed around the richly furnished room. A large walnut bed stood in the center of one wall, and a small rosewood desk was tucked neatly in an alcove beside it. The carpet, covering most of the floor, was a deep red color pattern with large pink roses and the walls were painted white, matching the white marble fireplace. Getting up, I walked over to the tall handsome bookcase, opened the glass doors, and ran my fingers over the smooth leather bookbindings. There was Dickens, Thackery, Shakespeare, and many others from which to choose. On a lower shelf, I discovered brand new editions of Keats, Shelly, and Wordsworth poems. I smiled as I closed the bookcase doors. Mr. Longdon surely provided food for the mind.

I picked my bonnet and shawl and hung them up in the wardrobe on the other side of the room, and unpacked my carpet bag. After doing that, it did not take me long to undress and crawl into the inviting feather bed. I blew out the lamp, and as I was settling myself down to sleep, I heard muffled laughter coming from the other room. I listened until all was quiet again, then rolled over on my side and soon drifted off to sleep and had a strange dream. I dreamt I was walking up and down the circular stairs with somebody who was invisible, and when I awoke in the morning, my limbs felt numb and heavy and I had to sit on the side of the bed massaging life back into them.

The fire in the fireplace had died down in the night and the room felt cold and unfriendly. Putting on my woolen robe and slippers, I went over to the grate and poked some smoldering coals alive again then going over to the tall bay window I opened the velvet drapes and looked down on a foggy gray-green lawn that stretched to the edge of a dark woods facing the east side of the house. Outside, all was gray-colored and silent under a leaden sky. Turning away from the dismal scene, I hurriedly washed and put on my dark-green silk dress with the white Irish lace collar. I wished to look my very best before meeting my new mistress. Glancing at the cupid clock on the mantelpiece, I heard a soft rap on the door. Mrs. Childs entered the room with my breakfast tray; it was exactly eight O'clock. "Good morning," she said. "Did you sleep well last night?" She gave me a cheery smile as she set the tray on a table near the fireplace. I returned her smile and said I had indeed slept well.

Completely famished, I eagerly drew up a chair to the little round table and, sitting down, spread the white linen napkin across my lap. The food smelled delicious. There were hot scones, and honey, sunny-faced eggs, and round fat sausages topped off with three kinds of cheese and steaming hot tea. Mrs. Childs stood off to one side watching me good-naturedly to the last bite, then she moved over to the connecting door and listened a while. "I think her ladyship is up now," she whispered, "if you are ready, I shall take you in and introduce you to her." I was relieved to hear her say that, for I certainly didn't relish the thought of barging in there all alone. I have always been a coward with strangers. Making myself presentable, I quickly smoothed my hair in the washstand mirror and straightened my lace collar. I was ready for Lady Longdon—I thought.

Mrs. Child tapped discreetly on the connecting door panel, and after a moment or so a dull voice told us to come in. I'll never forget my first impression of Lady Longdon. I had expected to meet a tall, imposing figure with snowy-white hair, but instead, when I entered that stuffy room, my eyes fell on a small wizened creature whose dark hair and eyes were so much like her son's. Mrs. Childs quietly introduced me. The tiny woman was crouched in a rocking chair swathed in woolen shawls, her pale wrinkled face set in a grim expression. She seemed to have no substance whatever; she reminded me of a crow sitting on a rail fence. Turning her dark eyes on me, she said, "So, you are Jennifer Marks, eh?" I felt I was being picked clean with the look she gave me. "Well," she went on, "you look more intelligent than some others I've seen lately. I cannot abide stupid people. I'm sure you understand what I mean?" Her haughty stare went right through me. Then, all at once, she clutched her bony chest and called for her bottle of medicine. Taking me aside, Mrs. Childs took a small brown bottle from the top of a dresser and handed it to me. She whispered in my ear, "You will get used to this... she's faking, of course, but just go along with it."

I took the bottle and a glass of water over to Lady Longdon and handed them to her. She glanced up at me piteously and quickly popped one of the small white pills in her mouth, (I found out later they were only sugar pills)and sighed with relief.

"I suppose my son has told you of my weak heart?" Lady London gazed at me steadily. I nodded my head. "Yes, I'm sure he did. I'm such a burden to John," she sighed. Extracting a handkerchief from the folds of her many shawls, she wiped her faded eyes. I failed to see a single tear anywhere.

Mrs. Childs had been taking this all in. She looked at her lady-ship and said, "Is there anything else you need, Lady Longdon?"

The tiny woman answered off-handedly, "No Sara, that will be all." She settled back in her rocking chair and closed her eyes.

Mrs. Childs turned and gave me a meaningful grin as she went out the door. I would not say I was the happiest young woman in the world at that moment for there were two things about Lady Longdon that made me nervous: first, there was her thin whining voice, and secondly her way of looking at one out of the corner of her eye. One could almost see her mind churning. The woman must have sensed my uneasiness, for she opened her eyes and told me to please sit down and stop looking at her; I supposed I had not taken my eyes off her face since I first entered the room. I took a chair opposite her and at once she began talking to me in a crisp tone. "Now look here, Jennifer Marks," she said, "haven't I already told you I cannot abide stupidity?" Lady Longdon stopped speaking and looked hard in my face. "Why do I make you nervous?" she asked out of a clear blue sky.

Luckily, I had gotten hold of myself. I laughed and assured her it was not so, saying I only felt strange starting a new post, that was all. Lady Longdon pursed her thin lips without comment; I never did know whether she believed me or not. We sat looking at one another for a while, then she asked me if I could write well. I thought she meant writing letters for her, but that wasn't it at all. She told me she wanted to write her autobiography but could not manipulate the pen on account of her arthritic hands. I had noticed earlier that she kept her gnarled hands hidden in her shawls. I nodded at her, saying I understood perfectly.

"I promise you some tasty morsels, Jennifer Marks," she said, half-closing her old dark eyes in thought. Coming out of her reverie, Lady Longdon sat up in her rocking chair and explained to me my duties as her companion, then just as abruptly, she ended the interview telling me to go to my room; she said she was tired and wanted to rest. I was more than happy to oblige.

❧   2   ☙

CHRISTMAS BRUSHED by me without a single greeting from anyone at the great hall. I thought this very odd. I learned, later on, why Christmas was never observed at Longdon Hall. I had always revered the Lord's birthday, and so did my family and friends back home, and my stepmother, evil disposition or not, had always offered us a peaceful and happy holiday each year. It was the only thing I missed from the old days. I spent my first Christmas at Longdon Hall, reading my bible and Dickens' Christmas Carol. Once, during the afternoon, I thought I heard footsteps pacing the gallery. I got up and opened my door, but nobody was there.

It was now the middle of January and for the last several weeks, Lady Longdon had been dictating her autobiography to me and my fingers were stiff and score writing so many words. She insisted on checking over every detail, sometimes changing a whole paragraph more to her liking. I must say the tiny woman had lived an exciting life if all she told me was true. Dark threads constantly crisscrossed brighter ones in her life story, and I strongly suspected most of the trials she said she suffered were of her own making. Lady Longdon seemed to exude trouble.

One afternoon after her ladyship dismissed me to my room, I eagerly settled down in my red-velvet easy chair to read and relax my thoughts, but I no sooner opened my book when there came a sharp rapping on the gallery door. I knew it wasn't Mrs. Childs, as she always rapped softly. Hurrying over to the door, I opened it and saw Mr. Longdon standing there smiling down at me with those wonderful dark eyes of his. "Forgive the intrusion, Miss Marks," he said quietly, "would you consider having dinner with us downstairs tonight?" he asked, "if you are free, that is," he hastily added. I thought he was listening for something, but perhaps I was imagining things. He searched my face, making me feel very important. I realized slowly that I would be delighted to have dinner with the family. Mr. Longdon smiled down at me again and suddenly I felt ware and protected; nobody had ever made me feel this secure, certainly not my father even in his best days. Still, I was cautious of Mr. Longdon. I remembered my first impression of him. There was something about the man I couldn't quite put my finger on, and it bothered me.

Mr. Longdon told me to come downstairs at six-thirty that evening, then he turned and walked around the gallery and I watched his tall figure disappear down the winding stairway. I thought I heard a door click shut somewhere. Closing my door, I returned to my chair and tried to concentrate on my book, but it was no use, for all I saw on the page was a pair of fascinating dark eyes staring into mine. The afternoon dragged by and soon it was time to dress and go downstairs. I looked in on Lady Longdon and found her asleep in bed shrouded in her shawls; she would not need me for the rest of the day. I decided to wear my dark-green silk and emerald brooch; it was my best dress, and I felt comfortable in it. I took one last glance at myself in the mirror and if not entirely thrilled at what I saw; I was not disappointed either, for my auburn hair shone like copper after my brushing it a hundred strokes. My eyes looked softer, too.

I began to feel uneasy as I went down the stairs. I wondered how the other members of the family would greet me. Would they feel embarrassed having an ordinary companion sitting at their dinner table? These thoughts worrying me. I came to the foot of the stairs and saw Mr. Longdon standing in the drawing-room doorway. He hurried toward me, smiling. Gallantly offering me his arm, he said, "Shall we go into the dining room?"

We walked down the hall and entered a sumptuous room. It was paneled in rich brown walnut wood and gold brocade, having a lofty beamed ceiling. I immediately noticed a large oil painting of a lovely young woman with two little boys and a little girl hanging on the wall. The woman's face was vaguely familiar, and I realized I was looking at Lady Longdon in her youth. The two boys at her knee were Mr. Longdon and his brother Robin; did they have a sister? Mrs. Childs hadn't mentioned their having one.

Mr. Longdon politely drew out a chair for me at the table and I sat down, then he walked to the head of the table and sat down too and we waited. Soon, the sound of footsteps came down the hall, and Uncle Thorne Longdon, and brother Robin entered the dining room. Mr. Longdon graciously introduced me to them, explaining that I was their dinner guest that night. Robin Longdon eyed me curiously as he sat down opposite me. He was alarmingly handsome with his thick golden wavy hair and amber eyes. Physically, he was a Greek God, but mentally, as I found out later, he was darkness itself. Giving me a glamorous smile, he murmured, "Welcome to our table, Miss Marks." He kept his golden eye on me all through the meal, and it's a wonder I did not drop my china teacup. Uncle Thorne rested his dim eyes on me and remarked how nice it was having an attractive young lady like me in their midst. I was highly flattered. I liked uncle Thorne. Not because of his nice compliment, but because he was a real gentleman.

I don't know yet how I managed to eat my first meal at Longdon Hall dinner table without dropping my fork and making a fool of myself. I was as nervous as a cat, wondering why Robin Longdon started at me so hard. I saw Mr. Longdon frown once or twice at his brother. The conversation flowed along interestingly enough and I learned that Longdon Hall was built in Elizabethan times. Uncle Thorne proudly informed me that an ancestor of theirs had been a favorite of the Virgin Queen, and she had presented him with a golden jewel box filled with precious jewels. It was an heirloom claimed by the eldest son of each generation down through the years. This story intrigued me. I said I would very much like to see the box sometime.

Robin spoke across the table to me as I was eating my dessert. He asked me how long I had been doing this work. I confessed that this was my first position as a companion. I kept my eyes on my plate, not meeting his bold gaze.

"Oh, is that so?" answered Robin, smooth as velvet. "Well, in that case, I consider Mother fortunate landing such a perfect one. Would you care for some more dessert?" he asked, passing me a silver tray of French pastry. I declined. One eye on his brother, Mr. Longdon said, "Miss Marks, if you are finished I would like to discuss some matters with you in the drawing-room." I nodded my head and, excusing myself, rose and pushed back my chair. Mr. Longdon joined me and we left the dining room.

After Mr. Longdon cased the sliding doors in the drawing-room, he turned to me saying, "Thank you, Miss Marks, for joining us tonight, from now on you will wind up with us, I can see no reason for your staying upstairs at dinnertime. Mother is usually in bed asleep at that hour, anyway." He turned and walked over to the tall arched window and stud with his back to me. He said, "I hope my bother did not upset you, I noticed the way he stared at you across the table, it was rid of him—but, that's Robin." Mr.

Longdon sounded resigned as if this was not the first time he had, had to explain his brother's actions. I told him to not give it another thought. I said Robin had not really offended me.

Mr. Longdon turned around and walked back to me, saying, "No, Miss Marks, perhaps not, but just the same I intend to keep my eye on that young man." And I knew he would do just that, for as he spoke, I saw a flicker of impatience cross his face. Mr. Longdon slid back the drawing-room doors and escorted me to the foot of the stairs. Smiling down at me, he bade me a soft good night, and I climbed the stairs light as a feather.

Spring came gently to Longdon Hall that year of 1860. Crocuses pushed their heads out of the moist earth and the tall elm trees on the driveway took on a shadowy green. The woods on the east side of the house had their own way of expressing the change in seasons with all kinds of new bird calls. It was about the mid week of April and I had been at Longdon Hall for about five months. I did not know Lady Longdon any better now than when I first met her. I found her to be a crafty, domineering woman. There wasn't a drop of kindness in her whole body unless it concerned Mr. Longdon. She idolized her oldest son, having little patience or time for Robin; I was aware of this the first month I was there. Yet, Mr. Longdon rarely visited his mother, and when he did, his attitude towards her was respectful and cool.

I remember the day he knocked at her door, bringing her a fancy new bed warmer from London. He had gone there on business for a few weeks. I remember his face lit up when I opened the door, and how awkwardly I backed away to let him pass by me into the room. I was so happy to see him at home again. Lady Longdon was curled up in her rocking chair, half-awake and half-asleep. Bu tween she caught sight of her son, she sat straight up and held out her thin arms, exclaiming, "Oh! John dear, you are home!" Mr. Longdon walked over to her and I saw how stiffly he bent down and kissed her cheek; I wondered about this. I wanted to leave mother and son alone to visit, but when I moved over to my doorway, Mr. Longdon stopped me. He said he wanted me to stay. I remember the sharp look Lady Longdon gave me but covered it up with a smile, saying it was all right for me to stay. To say I was embarrassed would be putting it mildly. Sitting on the edge of my chair, I listened to them discuss things that were far over my head. Lady Longdon questioned her son about expenses at the Hall and about servant problems. She asked if the grounds were in good shape and if the gardener had seeded the lawn early enough. Mr. Longdon patiently answered her questions. "John," she said, in a voice that seemed to come from her shoes, "I can always depend on you to get things done, can't I? Thank the good Lord you are not like Robin—I some-times wonder how he has made it this far—well. I washed my hands of him long ago," she declared coldly. "Adelaide knew what she was doing when she took little Marie and left him. He is just like his father." She sniffed and pursed her wrinkled lips in a straight line. Talking hold of Mr. Longdon's hand, she gazed up in his face and said, "Tell me, John, do I make you unhappy? Do you wish me dead and in my grave?"

Mr. Longdon's face tightened, and he snatched his hand away. I remember the way he answered her. "Stop talking nonsense mother, you are only working on my sympathy, and I'm afraid I haven't much to give you."

I focused my attention on the flowered wallpaper, trying to block out their words. Lady Longdon began a muffled sniffling, and once she glanced my way as if to say, *see how cruel he treats me?* I remember dropping my eyes to examine a loose thread in my skirt. I was not surprised to learn that Robin had a wife and child. It seemed to fit in somewhere. Mr. Longdon spoke again. He asked his mother if she had taken any exercise that day. I'll never forget the hurt look on Lady Longdon's face. "Why John," she said, "how can you say such a thing? You know I can hardly move around, let alone exercise. My poor old heart simply would not take it!" I recall the way she grabbed her chest and started gasping as though she were dying, and the nonchalant way Mr. Longdon stood looking down at her. I did not interfere, for I knew as well as Mr. Longdon that it was all put on. Lady Longdon was as strong as a horse. Our eyes met over her head, and I knew what he was thinking. We understood one another. Bidding us a curt good night, Mr. Longdon left the room. I remember he had no sooner closed the door when his Mother got up on her feet and walked back and forth across the room as if she were trying to prove something. It had not taken me very long to realize that Lady Longdon was no invalid. There was nothing wrong with her heart other than being cold and selfish.

I had continued eating my dinner downstairs; I especially enjoyed talking to Uncle Thorne. He and I became good friends. A former sea captain, he delighted me with tales of the far east and other interesting places he had visited. He spoke in a beautiful, dignified way and I hung onto every word; I liked him and I knew he liked me, too. As for Robin, I simply ignored him staring at me.

Spring quietly burst into glorious summer. The elm trees and the wide lawns were now in full dress, and the air was light and sweet with the scent of June roses. It was a far cry from the first night of my arrival at Longdon Hall. I had been frightened then. Feeling free and easy, I had gone outside one day in June for a walk. Lady Longdon had finished her autobiography two weeks before relieving me of some tiresome writing. I had taken down thousands of words of not much to do about anything, and after I had finished, she stacked the manuscript in a neat pile and shoved it into a dresser to gather dust, so now I was free to amuse myself most of the day. I never understood why Lady Longdon wanted a companion. As I rounded the east side of the mansion, I looked up at the sky. The sun was high and warm, reflecting the beautiful rose bushes lining the lawn. For some reason, I was drawn to the woods. I wanted to explore the place and there was no better time than now to do so. Crossing the lawn, I stepped over a low wooden barrier into the woods. My hoop skirt hampered me some, but I kept on going until I reached a small clearing.

A woodsy scent mingled with sweet honeysuckle permeated the little clearing. It was enchanting. Placing my hands on my hips, I filled my lungs with the refreshing air; it was a treat after being cooped up in Lady Longdon's bedroom for so many weeks. Although my shoes were damp from the wet ground, I strolled around examining the different species of wildflowers growing there so abundantly and I gathered a few to take back to my room. As I stepped over the low barrier onto the lawn, I heard somebody behind me. It was Robin Longdon.

"I see you are a nature lover, Miss Marks," he said, coming up beside me in that quick way of his.

I turned and looked at him. "You were in there too?" I sounded irritated, but he just laughed at me with a strange look in his eyes.

"Oh, I'm not above a stroll in the woods now and then," he replied. "It's good for one's soul, you know." I was certain he never had set foot in the woods before. I squelched the thought of him following me in there.

We crossed the lawn into the house, Robin running on about the Longdon estate. His prattling went in one ear out the other for good looks or not. Robin Longdon was negative as far as I was concerned.

He walked into the house with me to the foot of the stairs and stood grinning at me. I said politely, "You have reason to be proud of Longdon Hall, Mr. Longdon. It's a very beautiful place and I enjoy being a part of it."

Robin's expression changed. Digging his hands deep in his coat pockets, he stared at me a long time and said, "And we enjoy having you here, Miss Jennifer Marks." The words rolled off his tongue like syrup. I longed to be free of him, but he stood on the stairs in front of me, not moving an inch, and that irritated me. I don't know what I might have said to him had Mr. Longdon not appeared just then. Robin quickly stepped aside when he saw his brother. With a smile, Mr. Longdon said hello to me, making me feel safe and warm again. I pointed to the wildflowers I held in my hand, telling him I had taken a stroll in the woods.

"Yes, I see," he said softly, "we will have to tell Mrs. Childs to put them in a vase for you."

Mr. Longdon turned to his brother, questioning him. "Isn't this your day in town? I thought you would have left before this."

Robing shrugged his loose shoulders and glanced at his watch. I expected him to make a retort of some kind, but instead, he bowed to me and walked away. Mr. Longdon asked me if Robin made me nervous. I quickly told him no,

"Well, you appeared uneasy to me as I came along the hall."

I smiled at the man I loved. Yes, I had fallen in love with Mr. Longdon, without a shadow of a doubt. He laughed. "In that case, Miss Marks, I'll let you go and get back to my papers. There is no rest for the wicked, so they say."

I gazed up at him, my heart in my eyes, "You could never be wicked, Mr. Longdon," I murmured foolishly. Mr. Longdon suddenly walked away from me without a word,room, leaving me standing on the stairs biting my tongue for being so bold. When I reached my room, I flung the wildflowers on the table, my cheeks on fire. What an idiot I had been for daring to imagine that Mr. Longdon cared for me romantically; I was beneath him both socially and intellectually and I had better realize it. Coward that I was, I pleaded an upset stomach and did not go downstairs to dinner for several nights afterward. I simply could not face Mr. Longdon.

The days passed uneventfully into late summer, and every night at the dinner table I spoke hardly at all, keeping my eyes on my plate most of the time. I felt uncle Thorne watching me out of the corner of his eye, and when he spoke to me I answered him in a friendly way, wondering what was in Mr. Longdon's mind. He spoke to me only when he had to, which hurt me more than if he had not spoken at all. Robin continued his little game with me, but I just ignored it. I remember one evening at the dinner table; I had just finished up my cup of tea and glancing up I caught Mr. Longdon staring at me in a curious way, his dear eyes were hollow with dark circles under them and he looked very tired and upset and longed to rush over to him and take him in my arms, but of course, I could not.

Then one day, Lady Longdon sent me downstairs on an errand to Mrs. Childs. It had been another easy day for me as Lady Longdon, engrossed in a book, paid little attention to me. She would often draw into her shell and not speak to me for hours on end, as if I cared. I'm sure she wanted to be rid of me when she told me to go downstairs. As I opened her bedroom door, I saw Mr. Longdon coming around the gallery towards me and my heart skipped a beat at the sight of him. I wanted to avoid him, but he blocked my way and neither one of us uttered a word. I made a move to go around him, but he held me back.

"Jennifer, please," he whispered.

I do not know to this day how it all happened, but suddenly I was in his arms, and he pressed his lips on mine gently and hungrily, and I clung to him, my heart overflowing with love for him. Nevertheless, the overpowering emotion was laced with fear, not of him, but something else at Longdon Hall. I remember how my dear John held my shoulders and gazed down in my face pleading for my love, and how I laid my hand on his broad chest telling him I did indeed love him, and how he swept me in his arms kissing me again and again. We stood there a long time, then arm in arm walked around the gallery and down the winding stairway. When we reached the foyer, something made me turn around and look up at the fourth floor. Lady Longdon stood at the gallery railing staring down at us. I was glad John did not see her. We parted at the drawing-room doorway with another kiss.

I was afraid this was all a dream and that I would wake up as the very same person I had always been, but it was no dream. I was loved by Lord Longdon of Longdon Hall and the wonder of it struck me full force. I was so happy I could have burst as I walked down the hall to the kitchen area to see Mrs. Childs. After I delivered Lady Longdon's message, I smiled and said, "How nice you look today, Mrs. Childs." It was an inane remark, but I had to say something, for my heart was so full I wanted to spread happiness wherever I went.

I glanced at Mrs. Bevins, the cook, who stood at her stove arranging her pots and pans. "Hello Mrs. Bevins, and how are you today?" I asked cheerily. The nice old woman turned and nodded to me with a smile. She was round, sturdy, and loved to hum at her work. I loved talking to her just to listen to her thick Shropshire accent. I liked both of these women and I knew I had two allies should I ever need them. I heard Mrs. Childs laugh. "Miss Jennifer," she said, "her highness must be in a fine mood today by the look on your merry face." She reached out and patted my arm, and Mrs. Bevins joined in with, "Ah! That must be so."

I wondered what my friends would think had they known the reason for my cheerful attitude; I had an idea they would give me their blessings. I was urged to sit down and have a cup of tea with them, which I did. I left the kitchen—my head still in a spin—and went down the hall lingering in the foyer in hopes that John would appear again, but he was nowhere in sight.

When I reached my room, I drew a chair over to the window and gazed down at the splendid grounds of Longdon Hall. The first flush of excitement had gone out of me, and I began to see things more clearly. Was I falling into something I would regret? I had sense enough to realize that love could blind one to the hard facts of life, for I had seen this happen with my father. In his eyes, my stepmother was an angel and nothing less, and it did not seem to bother him how nasty she treated me as long as she stayed there under his roof taking care of him. I was simply a fixture in my father's house, and I suppose he was relieved when I left—how could I ever forgive him for that? Jerking myself back to the present, I sat analyzing the depth of my love for John Longdon. It was deep and good, and I knew it. It was a thought I had been gathered up in a soft warm cloud where nothing could ever touch me or harm me again. Still, if this was so, why did I feel afraid? I asked myself many questions as I sat there with my chin in my hands. A tiny wren suddenly perched itself on my windowsill, the little creature looked so frail and defenseless yet I knew just the same, that the little bird had a world of stamina under his smooth gray feathers; he could take care of himself under all conditions and so could I.

The afternoon sun was low in the sky. Glancing at the cupid clock on the mantle, I saw that it was almost dinnertime, and like it or not, a warm feeling ran through me at the thought of seeing John again. How strange it was to be in a world of love.

Everything had taken on new life for me—even the roses in the carpet looked alive and in my foolish way I could almost smell their perfume.

I put on my dark-green silk dress and a new yellow-lace collar, fastening it with a large amber brooch. I gazed in the mirror at my pink cheeks and sparkling eyes. Would the family guess my secret? Just then, I knew I had better check on her, so I opened the door and went in.

"Is there anything you want, Lady Longdon?" I asked politely.

Her ladyship gazed at me for a long time, then said, "I want a lot of things, Miss Marks, but nothing you could give me. Hand me that shawl over there. No, not that one! The blue one! It's so cold in here I could die." She looked at me narrowly. "You would like me to die, wouldn't you, missy?"

Shocked, I stood there gasping at her, not sure of my ground, then I found my tongue. "Why do you say that, Lady Longdon?" I said. "I have no reason to wish you dead. I only wish the best."

Not taking her black eyes off me, Lady Longdon arranged her shawl around her frail shoulders and said, "Now, that's neither here nor there, is it Miss Marks?" She waved her hand at me imperiously, ordered me to go downstairs to dinner, and would I please tell John that she wanted to see him that evening.

As I entered the dining room, I felt John's eyes upon me. I did not look up for fear I would give it all away. Uncle Thorne smile at me as I sat down and I smiled back. John threw me a warm glance from the head of the table, that said many things. The meal progressed quietly. Even Robin had little to say. Nellie, the young house-maid, brought in our tea as we were finishing up our dessert. I thought she was such a lovely creature with her jet-black hair and Irish-blue eyes. I noticed the pleading look she gave Robin as she poured his tea. He quickly looked the other way. I saw this same thing once before, but gave it no thought.

I sipped my tea and started talking to uncle Thorne. He told me his rheumatism was bothering him and that he had not slept well the night before; I told him I was sorry to hear that. He laughed and said at times he wished he could turn back the clock. I said, "But, uncle Thorne, just think what you have learned over the years. Young people have a disadvantage. They have to learn step by step, day by day, don't they?"

Uncle Thorne gave me a keen look. "Young woman," he said, "you've got a sensible head on those dainty shoulders of yours, and don't you dare lose it. Never trade your insight and intelligence for another's gift of gab, you know what I mean?" He gave Robin a sidelong glance, and I caught on right away. Uncle Thorne knew his nephew backwards and forwards, and I suspected he also knew all that went on at Longdon Hall. Did he know about John and me? After dessert, John leaned back in his chair and gazed around the table, a broad grin on his face.

"I wish to make an announcement," he said, glancing first at me and then at the rest of them. "Miss Marks and I are going to be married." I was stunned. John had not asked me to marry him. Never-the-less, the idea set very well with me, yet I still wondered why John did it this way. Robin stared at this brother, then at me and burst out laughing. Apparently, he considered the idea a huge joke. John did not, for he slapped his hand down hard on the table and cried, "That's enough, Robin! I fail to see what's so funny."

Robin got a hold of himself. "My dear brother," he began, stiffly, "I'm sorry for being such a clod. I cannot picture you a married man, not even in the widest stretch of my imagination." Turning to me, he said, "I meant no reflection on you, my dear Miss Jennifer. It's just the idea of my brother marrying anybody at all that strikes me as funny. My mother has kept a tight leash on John for a good many years, and she will not loosen it now." Robin eyed his brother across the table. "By the way,' he said, slowly, "have you mentioned this to our dear mother yet?" John did not answer Robin; he gave me a warm look instead then finished his dessert.

Uncle Thorne looked sharply at Robin and said, "You ought to learn to keep your mouth shut. If John wishes to marry this nice young lady, they have my blessings all the way, and I don't give a hoot whether your mother likes it or not." He reached over and patted my hand; I could have kissed him for that. Robing pulled a sour face, not saying anymore. Leaving the dining room, John took hold of my arm and steered me down the hall into the drawing-room and closed the sliding doors. He gathered me in his strong arms and kissed me hard on the lips. Recovering my breath, I asked him why he had not warned me about the announcement. Smiling down in my face in a fatherly way, he replied, "My little Jennifer, if I had, I'm afraid you would have backed out of marrying me, so, announcing it at the table was the only way to be sure of you, you see? How could you refuse me in front of the others"?

I remember the warm glow of happiness that shot through me at the thought of becoming John's wife. I don't know when John told his mother he was going to marry me, or what was said, but I do know I got up the next morning feeling like a brand new person. I was so happy I could have soared straight out of the window and joined the birds.

As I was getting dressed, I heard Lady Longdon call to me through the door panel, "Jennifer," she cried, "will you please come in here?" I hurriedly buttoned up my dress and took a fresh handkerchief out of the pink-satin box on my dresser and tucked it in my belt, then opened her door. She was standing at the window, gazing down on the rain-washed lawn and driveway. It was a gray depressing day, the kind that comes along in the early fall and seeps into one's bones; I was too happy to notice it, though.

"Sit down," said Lady Longdon, keeping her arched back to me. I took a chair and waited. Turning around, the diminutive woman looked at me disdainfully and said, "Whatever gave you the idea you would be a suitable wife for my son, John?" Her mood was mean and nasty.

"Why... I... ah..." I tried to tell her I loved John, but she cut me off.

"Never mind trying to explain yourself," she snapped, "you are a little nobody from nowhere, and if you think I'm going to let go of my John, you are badly mistaken. I happen to be his mother, and his first duty is to me." She walked toward me; her face pale and angry, then suddenly she clutched her chest and sat down. I got her medicine bottle and gave her a glass of water. After she had taken her pill, she looked up at me and told me to get out of her room. I hesitated, and tried to tell her again that I really loved John, but she turned on me and said, her voice as cold as a blade of steel, "Please get out of here." I went back to my room and sat down. Robin was right about his mother.

I did not see John for about a week after that, as he had gone away again on business. It was perfectly clear that Lady Longdon did not want my company, so I spent my time reading books. I could not go out for a walk on the grounds, as the weather continued cold and damp, and the fact that John had not said goodbye to me did not help matters. Mrs. Childs brought a tray of tea up to my room every afternoon and I looked forward to it. She was such warm company, I just loved talking to her, and not once did she mention Lady Longdon, yet I'm sure she suspected I was having difficulty with her. One day she brought me a newspaper and said to me, in her usual kindly way, "Here ye are, dearie. I thought maybe you would like to know what's going on outside this old pile of bricks." I remember the way she looked at me like I was her own daughter and blurted out, "Ah! Now, don't ye fret about Mr. Longdon. He will soon be home and ye'll perk up like a pretty morning glory." I knew right then and there that Mrs. Childs understood everything.

John returned late on a rainy afternoon. I stood at the window watching his carriage come up the drive, and my silly heart started bouncing around. Deciding I would go downstairs and greet him, I quickly appraised myself in the mirror. I saw an entirely different person; there was a soft sweet expression around my large mouth and a new light in my hazel eyes. I hoped that John would notice this change in me. So eager was I to feel his warm arms around me again, I ran down the stairs, almost losing my footing. When I reached the end of the stairs, I saw John come in the front door, his overcoat wet with rain; he did not notice me standing on the stairs; I watched him hang up his coat and hat and stand with his thumbs hooked in his vest pockets, staring at the floor. Taking a small white card out of his pocket, he studied it a long time, then put it back again. Something bothered him and I wondered what it was. I drew back in the shadow of the stairway for a while. Robin appeared in the hallway and he did not notice me either, as the foyer was dim.

Robin greeted John affably. "Well, home again, eh? I hope you had a good trip." He stared at John, his eyes half-closed.

"Yes," John soberly replied.

Robin strolled over to him and touched him on the arm. "Still going to marry the little companion?"

John frowned, annoyed, "Robin," he said, "I wish to God you would mind your own business, surely you have enough problems of your own to keep you busy." Meeting Robin eye to eye, he added, "I told you before, I'm going to marry Jennifer didn't I? Now, that's all I want to hear about it."

I stepped forward on the stairs and John saw me. Coming over to me, he caught me up in his arms and kissed me. (Robin had done back down the hall not seeing this.) John led me by the hand into the drawing-room and we sat down together on the green-velvet sofa. I asked him why he had not said goodbye to me before he left, and he told me he had left the house in such a hurry he completely forgot about me. I did not appreciate hearing this. I realized he had pressing responsibilities; but as long as he was back home with me now, nothing else mattered.

John tilted my chin and said, "Jennifer, I want to marry you right away. Perhaps next week, if it can be arranged." Looking up into his commanding dark eyes, I completely melted. What else could I say but yes? "Jennifer, I don't mean to push you into this," explained John, "it's just that I need you so much."

"I understand, John," I whispered back. Drawing me close, he kissed my face and my hair, and we sat there for a long while. I remember how loudly the clock ticked in the bing silent room, and how happy I knew that John's life would be my life from now on.

❦ 3 ❦

THE FOLLOWING WEEK, John and I were quietly married at a little chapel nearby, on a cloudy, rainy day. I wore my silk dress, and carried a bouquet of yellow roses, a gift from John. Robin and Mrs. Childs were our witnesses, and Robin eyed me throughout the ceremony, making me very nervous; I was relieved when it was all over with and we were back at Longdon Hall. Lady Longdon had made no demands on me since our last conversation, nor had she called for John to come up to see her. However, he tried to see his mother before we left for the chapel that day. She refused to open her door to him.

When I got back to the Hall, I immediately moved my things downstairs to John's apartment on the second floor. I remember how awkward and shy I felt hanging my few garments next to his in the large wardrobe in his bedroom. John's bedroom was long and wide, furnished comfortably with a high canopied bed and two chests of drawers in dark walnut wood. There was an uphol-stered armchair next to a big round table upon which stood a handsome green-glass lamp. My eye caught the high, plump feather mattress on the bed, covered with a red-brocade cover-let. I glanced away, concentrating my attention on the heavy lace curtains hanging so luxuriously on the high windows and the green satin drapes on either side. It was strictly a masculine room, and I felt strange in it, yet I certainly belonged there now that I was John's wife. I could have shouted for joy!

I sat down in the armchair gazing at John's pipe and tobacco pouch laying on the table beside a collection of odd shaped wooden blocks that looked as though they might be part of a game. My John was a down-to-earth man. His surroundings proved that. Getting up, I went over and peeked in a smaller room opening off the bedroom. It had only a wide desk cluttered with papers and ledgers, and a tall bookcase in it. Apparently, John used this room for keeping his accounts; I went back and sat down. Fondly kissing me after the ceremony, John informed me he was leaving me on business for a few hours. "This is quite important, my little one," he said. "I shall be home before dinnertime." He gently stroked my flushed cheek with his finger, and I did not know whether to laugh or cry. "Robin and Mrs. Childs will take you back to the hall. Meanwhile, I want you to move your things downstairs to my quarters on the second floor."

I'll never forget the warm glow in John's dark eyes as he said this to me. I was disappointed, though, at his leaving me so soon after our wedding. What could be more important to him than me at that moment? I sat thinking about it until the shadows closed in on me. Getting chilly, I went over and closed the window drapes and coaxed some warmth back into the dying hearth, then lighted the green-glass lamp; I thought it was such a lovely lamp glowing like an emerald in its flickering flame. Glancing idly at the bronze clock on John's bedside table, I saw that it was 6 p.m. almost dinnertime, and John wasn't back yet. I had much to learn about my John, his strange turn of mind which could drive me mad one moment with uncertainty, and to the heights the next, but all this came later. I snuggled down in John's big soft chair and falling asleep, woke up with his lips on mine in a tender kiss. Towering over me, he pulled me to my feet and kissed me again in a more deliberate way and I clung to him, my head spinning. After a while, he let me go and said, "Let's go down to dinner, little one." Taking my hand, he led me out of the room and down the winding stairway.

Time passed happily for those first few weeks. John was sweet and thoughtful, I could not have asked for a more kind and considerate husband, still, there seemed to be something missing in our relationship, and more than that, whenever I caught his eye, he would glance away as though he were guilty of something, however, when I overlooked this; I loved John completely and I'm sure he realized it.

One day, about a month after we were married, I was sitting in a high-backed chair in the drawing room in front of the fireplace reading a book, when I heard voices out in the hall. I listened.

"Well, old boy, I suppose you went to Essex this week?" Robin asked.

I heard my John reply evenly, "Yes, I did, but why are you so interested?"

"Oh, I don't know," said Robin, "maybe it's because Lucille was such a beauty, and I liked her." I sat up in my chair.

John was silent, then he said, "I know, I know." I thought he sounded kind of sad, and I wondered jealously who Lucille was. A helpless feeling began to spread over me as I strained my ears to hear more. Robin spoke again.

"You would have married Lucille if mother had only kept her nose out of it. By the way, how is Lucille? Any worse?"

"No, thank God," replied John, "she seems to be holding her own, but with her heart, who knows? She is so thin and frail, it scares me just looking at her."

Robin blurted out recklessly, "John, give me the truth now. You are still in love with Lucille, aren't you?" Biting down hard on my lip, I heard John answer yes. The two of them came into the drawing-room, and I slid down in my chair out of sight. "But what about little Jennifer?" continued Robin softly. I was surprised he was concerned. Grasping the arms of my chair, I listened again. Slow at answering, John said, "What about Jennifer? Strange, you should ask that. She is my wife, isn't she?"

"I know Jennifer is your wife," said Robin, "but don't you think she deserves something more than that? You say you don't love her then why did you marry her? Are you trying to get back at mother?"

"I don't care to discuss it any further," returned John, his voice fading out in the foyer. Robin laughed, following him out the door.

I sat numb and cold in my chair. My hands shook, and I felt as though somebody had slammed a door in my face. The whole thing did not make any sense, and the more I thought about it, the more upset I became. Choking back my tears, I got up and walked out into the foyer and stood gazing up at the remote skylight, trying to get myself together. All of a sudden, Lady Longdon opened her door and came out on the gallery. She stood at the railing, staring down at me, laughing. I quickly grabbed my shawl off the hall table and hurried out the front door and down the steps, not knowing or caring where I was headed. I remember crossing the lawn and walking down the driveway in the rain until I reached the gate, and there I stood trying to decide whether I should run away from Longdon Hall or go along as if nothing had happened. I finally decide it would be foolish of me to let John suspect I knew anything about his friend Lucille. I hated the sound of her name. She had no place in his life now; he was my husband, and I vowed I would keep him no matter what.

I have a quieter frame of mind, my head and shoulders soaked with rain. I walked back to the house and as I climbed the steps, John opened the front door. He looked down at me, his eyes tired and heavy.

"Jennifer," he scolded, "what are you doing out in this rain? Do you want to catch pneumonia?" John smiled, but I knew he was annoyed seeing me in such a state. We went inside, and he removed my wet shawl and hung it up, then led me into the drawing-room and we sat down together before the roaring fire-place. My hands were icy cold and so was my heart. I gazed at my husband's handsome profile and his dark wavy hair. I almost broke down.

John sat preoccupied, and I held out my hands to the warm fire. My dress was limp and damp. I felt miserable inside and outside. John looked at me and said, "Jennifer, you had better go upstairs and put on some dry clothes. Mrs. Childs will bring you some hot tea." Slipping his arms around my shoulder, he kissed my cheek. "What's troubling you, little one?" he asked. "It's not like you to go walking around in the rain with only a shawl around your shoulders."

I avoided John's eyes. "I needed some exercise," I explained. "I did not realize the weather was so bad until I got outside." John continued looking at me, then he patted my arm and told me to run along upstairs and change. Without another word, I got up and went up to our bedroom and after drinking two cups of the hot tea Mrs. Childs brought me, I curled up in John's chair in my flannel robe thinking things over again, I did not want to go downstairs again that night not even for dinner. I had lost my appetite.

John came up about eight p.m. and I pretended to be absorbed in the book I was reading. I heard him walk across the room and back again. He said to me, "Why didn't we see you at dinner-time, Jennifer? Are you ill? Look at me." His tone was sharp.

Dropping the book in my lap, I raised my eyes, trying to think of some good excuse. John frowned down at me, saying, "What's bothering you, anyway? Come on Jennifer, what is it?"

I grasped the first thing that crossed my mind. "I guess I'm homesick," I answered lamely.

John laughed. "Homesick? My dear girl," he said, "from what you have told me of your family, I doubt it very much." He bent down and gave me a fatherly kiss on the cheek. "You are an odd little thing, but I love you nonetheless."

I cringed. John did not notice it though. Taking a chair beside me, he told me of Robin getting word that his wife Adelaide and his daughter Marie were coming back home. I was surprised hearing it. I said, "Oh, is that so? I imagine Robin likes the idea."

John grunted and filled his pipe with more tobacco. "Well. He should like it. Adelaide is a fine woman, and much too good for that philandering brother of mine. I'm surprised she wants to have anymore to do with him after the last breakup. This is not their first separation. She's left him several times before, but what beats me is why she always comes back again. Their daughter Marie is ten and a precocious little miss, but very beautiful." I was glad somebody was coming to Longdon Hall. It would give me something to else to think about besides Lucille. I picked up my book and started reading again. John did not stop me. He sat puffing on his pipe, seemingly in another world. Glancing up once, I caught him staring at me as though I were someone he did not know. Laying the book on the table, I took off my robe and went to bed, with visions of John and Lucille in my head.

Christmas slipped by joylessly and without fanfare. Robin's wife and daughter arrived at Longdon Hall after the new year. I immediately became friends with Adelaide. She was about twenty-nine but seemed older because she was so self-contained and wise as to the ways of people and the world. I had taken up needlepoint as a hobby, and she, china painting, and we spent many enjoyable hours together in the drawing-room pursuing our craft. I did not take to her daughter Marie nearly as well, for she acted wise beyond her years putting on airs and strutting about; and, as John had remarked, Marie was undoubtedly a beautiful child. She had Robin's golden wavy hair and his amber eyes, which I assure you missed nothing. Being tall for her age, Marie could have easily passed for fifteen and needless to say, Robin adored her and she him. I often watched her smiling and fawning over him at the dinner table, completely ignoring her mother. Robin did not try to catch my eye across the table as before. His daughter kept him too busy for that.

John and I got along together, sometimes pleasantly and sometimes silently. He still went off on his trips to Essex, never explaining a thing to me, and I never questioned him. I often wondered what he would have done had he realized I knew who he visited on these trips. I cannot say, in those early days, that John neglected me, for there were times when he treated me kindly. He brought me little gifts from Essex wrapped in fancy gold paper; the first time he did this I was so upset I almost threw the present in his face, but I soon learned to control my fits of jealousy and smile at him, hoping he would soon break away from the mysterious Lucille. I very seldom saw Lady Longdon, though one day about six months after John and I were married, Mrs. Childs told me the old lady wanted to see me. I recall how nervous I felt as I climbed up to the fourth floor gallery and knocked on her door. I hardly recognized the woman when she opened the door. She appeared so much stronger and less dependent. After I entered her room and sat down, Lady Longdon assumed her usual mean expression and began, "Well, Jennifer, you already know my sentiments concerning you and my son. Nevertheless, I must recognize the fact that you are John's wife, and make the best of it." Sweeping me from head to toe, she bluntly asked me if I was pregnant. I felt my face grow hot as I slowly shook my head. "Humn, all well and good then," she said tartly, "But, that's not to say you won't be in the future. Nature will out, you know, if it happens," she continued crisply, "I expect you to let me know at once so that I can arrange things properly. I mean the christening and all that. Above all, the family name must be protected. You must cooperate a hundred percent. Now, if it's a boy, his name shall be John, and if it is a girl, she will be named Lucille."

I went cold hearing the name Lucille. I stuttered. "Believe me, Lady Longdon, I have not given child-bearing much thought..."

She cut me off with a nasty laugh, "Well young lady," she retorted, her dark eyes sweeping my figure again, "you had better start thinking about it, you understand what I mean?" She smirked at me as though I had no sense at all, and I'll always remember the haughty way she walked over to the door and stood with her scrawny hand on the knob. "That's all I wanted to say to you," she declared loftily, "when you go downstairs please tell Adelaide and Marie to come up here. I want to talk to them."

I quickly brushed past her out the door; Lady Longdon had put uneasy thoughts in my head, thoughts I wanted to ignore. I met Adelaide in the foyer and told her what Lady Longdon had said to me. She took hold of my hand saying, "Now listen Jennifer, don't you pay any attention to that old lady. She tried her game with me years ago, and it just did not work. When Robin and I were first married, she made my life absolutely miserable watching my every move and ordering me about as though I had no mind of my own, this was long before she started playing invalid, but I asserted myself one day and since then she had little to say to me and I to her." Adelaide shook her head at the fourth floor and signed, "I wonder if she realizes what she does to people? Sometimes I feel sorry for her, then I think of what she did to John and Lucille and I... Oh! Sorry dear, I shouldn't have mentioned that."

I blinked a couple of times, mumbling that Lady Longdon wanted to see her and Marie. "Hmm, that's unusual," said Adelaide. "I wonder what she's got up her sleeve?"

Marie strolled out of the drawing-room just then and stood looking at us. "Who's got what up whose sleeve?" she asked boldly.

Adelaide frowned at her. "Never you mind," she said, "your grandmother wants to see us, and watch your tongue while you are up there."

Brushing past me without a word or a glance, Marie bounded up the winding stairway two at a time, Adelaide scolding her all the way. I turned and walked down the long hall to the kitchen, sorely in need of a talk and a cup of tea with Mrs. Childs. The warm kitchen seemed another world to me and I loved to go there. Mrs. Childs was seated at the table going over some kind of household reports, and Mrs. Blevins was in her usual place in front of the huge range preparing meat for meat pie. And how I loved that delicious meal. I smiled and said hello to my fiends. Mrs. Childs glanced up at me. "Ah! It's Miss Jennifer!" she exclaimed, her broad beaming smile lifted me up as nothing else could. She eyed me closely. "Are ye feeling well, my dear? Ye look kind of pasty to me."

I laughed, saying I felt fine and that I would enjoy a cup of tea with her and Mrs. Bevins. "Hurry, Annie! Get the tea things on the table, before Miss Jennifer gets away," said Mrs. Childs, pulling me down in a chair beside her. Soon, the three of us were sipping tea together as though we were old friends. I remember how secure I felt in their home-spun presence. I suppose they filled a gap in my life.

Mrs. Childs timidly asked, "Tell me child, are ye happy being Lady Longdon's daughter-in-law?"

I sat stirring my tea, afraid to look at her for fear she would guess the truth. Smiling at her, I answered lightly that I was truly happy and contented in my marriage.

"Ah! That is good," said Mrs. Childs, patting my hand, "a finer man never lived that Mr. John, and had his share of trouble too..." She broke off abruptly and turned to Mrs. Bevins, "Annie," she said, "are ye sure ye put enough spices in that concoction you are cooking over there? Ye know, Mr. Thorne likes the meat pie spicy."

Mrs. Bevins eyed her friend good-naturedly. "Go and taste it for yourself, Sara Childs," she replied.

I finished my second cup of tea, our conversation ranging from the weather to Adelaide and Marie. Mrs. Childs, not being the least vindictive or gossipy, warned me to watch what I said in front of Marie. "She is a strange one, she is," commented Mrs. Childs. "I've seen that you one behave like an angel in front of the family and like a devil when she was alone. Marie repeats all she hears to her father. Ah, but there now, it's none of my business, is it Miss Jennifer? The only reason I mentioned it is because I think a lot of ye, and I don't want to see ye hurt."

I said I would remember it. I knew Marie was an odd child who would bear watching. Standing up, I thanked my dear friends for the tea and said I would see them again soon. Mrs. Childs kissed me on the cheek. "If ye should ever need me, my dear," she said, "just push one of the buzzers and I'll come running." For some reason, a cold chill ran down my spine. Mrs. Childs was smiling, but she knew something.

I left the kitchen and went down the long, dim hall. As I crossed the foyer to the drawing-room, I felt a heavy hand on my shoulder; thinking it was John, I turned around and came face to face with Robin. He pulled me in his arms and kissed me hard on the lips, struggling and twisting. I could not break his hold on me. I could hardly breathe. He held me so tight. Turning furious—I did not have red hair for nothing—I finally squirmed free. "You fool! Have you completely lost your senses?" I fumed, shoving him away from me.

His face was chalk white. Robin stood in front of me searching me with his wild amber eyes, "Jennifer, Jennifer, don't be cruel," he whispered hoarsely, "I've loved you... ever since you first stepped in Longdon Hall, I can't help it, darling."

I quickly turned around, afraid that John might be standing there witnessing this, but nobody was around. Trying to compose myself, I said to Robin, "Do you realize what you are saying to me?"

Robin's mouth tightened. "Yes! I realize what I'm saying to you, and what's more, I don't give a damn! I don't love Adelaide, and I know John doesn't love you and..."

Having heard enough of his nonsense, I cut him off sharply. "That's enough, Robin! I advise you to straighten yourself out where I am concerned. I happen to be John's wife and he loves me no matter what you say or think." I swung around and went into the drawing-room, closing the door behind me. When I got inside, I dropped down in a chair near the door, clutching my woolen shawl tightly around me. I burned with humiliation. Robin had made me feel cheap, and I would never forgive him for it. Suddenly, I heard somebody across the room snickering. Then Marie bobbed up on her knees on the sofa and gazed at me with amusement. She had evidently seen everything. My heart almost stopped. Clambering over the back of the velvet sofa showing her lace pantalettes, she strolled over to me, a smirk on her pretty face. "You like my papa, don't you, Jennifer?" she asked. I did not answer her. Tossing her head,eye she continued haughtily, "Oh, well, if you don't want to discuss it, then neither do I."

We eye one another, "Marie," I replied carefully, "I have no idea what you are talking about." Eager to steer him off the subject, I suggested our playing a game of cards. Marie gave me a cold no. Siding closer to me, she whispered slyly, "Jennifer, I promise I won't tell uncle John if you will give me that pretty emerald brooch you wear." The child stood fiddling with a strand of her lovely blond hair, appraising me with half-closed eyes. Shocked at her boldness, I took her by the shoulders and steered her out in the foyer, telling her to run along and play. Shaking herself free, Marie flounced down the hall toward the kitchen; when she got about half-way she turned around and spat back at me, "I saw you and my papa kissing, and you needn't try to deny it either!" She took off like a shot, disappearing somewhere in the rear of the house.

❧

Weeks passed, and the grounds of Longdon Hall began to shimmer with another spring. How I loved springtime there. I remember the sweet tangy smell of it brushing my face as I threw open our bedroom window each morning. In those far-off days, I experienced magic and mystery in that stately mansion and looking back on it now, I sometimes wonder how I survived. I loved the place, but hated it too. Youth has a way, however, of surmounting obstacles, and I had my share of them with Lady Longdon, Robin, Marie, and not to say the least, Lucille. It was a good thing I steeled myself or else I might have had a far different story to tell. Mealtime was the worst, for I had to constantly shift my eyes, avoiding Marie's impudent stares and Robin's probing glances. Aside from that, I suppose one could say I was contented being married to John Longdon but; I needed much more than content to keep me happy. I needed John's mind and his love, Lucille had both.

John and I were married about six months when I realized I was going to have a child. I was thrilled and happy about it. Lady Longdon's imperious remarks to me concerning children had struck a nasty chord in me, making me coldly determined she should not know about my condition; but since I rarely saw the woman, my baby probably would be born without her knowing it. This is the way I hoped it would be.

One bright afternoon, I joined Adelaide in our favorite nook in the drawing room for a game of cards. We often relaxed this way or instead went for a walk on the grounds. This afternoon, my dear friend eyed me curiously as I crossed the spacious room towards her. "Why Jennifer," she exclaimed. "You look positively radiant. You're different somehow." Her turquoise eyes held mine as I sat down opposite her. I recall how Adelaide pursed her mouth and cocker her head trying to figure me out. "Well, how stupid I am!" she cried, bringing her hands down on the table. She leaned across the table and whispered, "you're going to have a little Longdon, aren't you?"

I blushed and nodded my head, happy she had guessed my secret, but I would have told her, anyway.

"Does John know about it yet?" grinned Adelaide.

"Not yet. I'm going to mention it to him tonight."

Adelaide picked up the cards and started shuffling them back and forth. I can still see her soft smiling face as she dealt the cards one by one on the table. Then, sobering a bit, she remarked, "I imagine John's mother will put on a show when she hears it."

I shrugged. "Truthfully, Adelaide," I replied. "I don't care one way or the another whether she does or not."

Adelaide gave me a sharp glance. "Thats good. I'm so glad you feel that way. Don't you tell her, let her guess."

"I intend to," I answered firmly.

We played a few games of Rummy, then decided to sit in front of the fireplace and chat a while. I rang for tea and we settled down on the long green sofa, happy in each other's company. If I had, had a sister I would have wanted her patterned after Adelaide Longdon, for a no sweeter personality could have been found on this earth. I loved her very much and when I think about her now, after all these years, the same warm comfortable feeling comes over me. Sometimes, I can almost hear her say, "Hello, Jennifer." Mrs. Childs brought us our tea. Setting the tray down on the table, she put her hands on her ample hips and smiled down at us saying, "It's nice to see your pretty young faces light up at the sight of me, now, I wonder if it's me or the tea?"

Adelaide and I giggled and said it was the tea, of course. Mrs. Childs chuckled going out of the room. I did the honors pouring the tea, and as I handed Adelaide her cup, I was suddenly struck with her sharply defined profile, delicate white skin. And dark-brown hair. I recall the turquoise-silk dress she word that day and how it accented her unusual blue-green eyes. I thought how blind and stupid Robin was for not appreciating her. What ailed him anyway? Was it vanity? Was he afraid of not being attractive to other women? I had noticed this male weakness in my father. My father was a handsome man and foolish too. I sometimes wondered how my mother ever lasted, with her plain honest face and red hair, there must have been times when she was ready to leave him. I was too young then to notice my parents. It was only after she died I noticed my father had dyed his hair brown and was acting like a schoolboy.

Adelaide must have read my thoughts about her looks. For she turned to me and remarked, "You have such pretty hair, Jennifer. That shade of green you are wearing brings out its highlights." Reaching out, she touched the bun on the back of my neck. "Why don't you try wearing your hair in ringlets? I think they would make you look very pretty." I had always worn my hair swept back in a severe style. Perhaps I would try the ringlets sometime. What did I have to lose? I sipped my tea, a warm glow spreading through me. I even felt pretty. When one is young, exterior things mean so much; Adelaide's kind remark had lifted me to the sky. I sat sipping my tea, wondering how many times John had compared me to Lucille in his mind. Robin had commented on her good looks. Well, maybe I would meet that mysterious lady sometime and judge for myself.

"Hey, Jennifer, where are you?" Adelaide's soft voice broke in on my thoughts. Setting her teacup but down in its saucer, she looked at me and smiled. I smiled back at her, explaining that I had just been thinking of something unimportant. "Well," laughed Adelaide, "if it's unimportant, just shoo it away." How I wish I could! I thought as I gazed lazily into the fire. I remember how silently we sat together on that green-velvet sofa in front of the crackling fire, which spat out sparks against the brass screen like miniature fireworks.

Adelaide spoke. "I suppose I shouldn't bring this up, but has John ever told you about Lucille Merridith? John and Lucille were engaged to be married about fifteen years ago, until Lady Longdon broke them up. Lucille was a lovely girl, but delicate. There was something wrong with her heart and I believe she died soon after. John's mother, hateful as she is, made up all kinds of nasty stories about Lucille. John, only twenty at the time, swallowed them whole, and that was the end of that. According to Robin, John became morose afterwards, absolutely soured on women, until you came along. He must love you very much, Jennifer."

Every nerve in my body tightened up like a spring, and I must have shown it, for Adelaide flung her arms around my neck and kissed me on the cheek. "Oh, Jennifer," she apologized, "please forgive my big mouth. I didn't mean to hurt you. I just wondered if you know about Lucille, that's all." Forcing a stiff smile, I told her to forget it. I said John belonged to me much more now than he ever had to Lucille. I added that I was sorry the girl had died. And at that moment, I hoped she would die and get out of my way. Adelaide nodded her head, searching my face, which I hoped didn't give me away.

"I knew you would say something nice like that," she said. "You are a sweet understanding soul Jennifer. I hope John never lets go of you." Yes. I certainly hoped he wouldn't either. Only time would tell.

We started talking of other things. Adelaide confided what a handful Marie was getting to be. "If I only knew how to communicate with the child," she said, staring into the fire. "I would feel so much better, but nothing I say makes sense to her. Marie thinks I'm totally unnecessary in her life and she is so bound up with her father, it's pitiful, and he gives into her." Adelaide paused. "Oh, it's not that I begrudge Robin her attention and love. That wouldn't be fair. It's only that I think I deserve some recognition." I remember how angry I felt with Marie that day. I could have cheerfully wrung her pretty little neck for causing Adelaide heartache. I still cannot look at a flickering hearth without seeing Adelaide's sweet sad face and hearing her say, "Oh, it's not that I begrudge Robin her attention..."

Reaching out, I took Adelaide's small hand in mine and told her that most girls went through a phase of *father adoration*. I said it would pass and not to worry about it. I could say this for I too, had adored my father and believed I was his whole life, and I suppose I was, until my stepmother appeared on the scene.

Adelaide smiled at me and said, "You're very wise, Jennifer, for one so young."

We sat talking until the fire died down to a rosy glow, then went in to dinner. Wanting to retire early—John was away again—I went upstairs soon after dinner and settled down to read. I guess after a half an hour passed when I heard excited voices coming from the fourth floor gallery. I got up and stepping outside. I looked up to see what was going on. I heard Adelaide say rather sharply, "Lady Longdon, please don't scold Marie. I know she's a bold child, but she was only trying to get your attention by pounding on your door that way. She needs recognition from you, as we all do; I cannot understand why you keep us all at arm's length. I'm well aware that John is your favorite, but I do wish you would consider our feelings, too."

"Well now! Isn't that just too bad!" cried Lady Longdon, her thin voice ringing out in the rotunda. "Neither you, nor Robin, nor your offspring matter to me in any way, shape, or form. Is that clear?" I heard her door slam shut. Adelaide ran around the gallery to the stairway and, to my horror, slipped and fell down the stairs to the third floor landing. I raced up the stairs and found my dear friend wedged in the curve of the stairs, her pretty head twisted toward the wall. What a horrible time that was! I can still see Robin taking the stairs two at a time from the first floor, and Marie standing in the middle of the foyer staring up at us wide eyed.

Somehow, Robin and I managed to carry Adelaide's limp body downstairs and lay it on the foyer floor, then Robin rushed out the door to get the doctor. Marie stood gawking down at her mother without a word or making a move toward her, but she laid perfectly still and that's the way it was. The doctor told us later that Adelaide had died instantly from a broken neck.

We buried my beloved friend in the family plot near the woods. It was the saddest day of my life; I could not control my grief. I needed John at my side, but he did not return home until it was all over. How I despised Lady Longdon after that. I would stand in the foyer looking up at her door wishing she would die too, but of course, she didn't. I was sure she planned on living forever, just to spite us. When John got home and I told him of Adelaide's death, he paced our bedroom floor back and forth, back and forth, upsetting me, so I almost screamed. Finally, he came to a stop in front of me and stared down at my face. He said, "Marcy died the very same way."

I frowned up at him. "I don't understand, John."

"My sister! My sister!" he cried impatiently, swinging away from me. He went on with the story. "It happened on a Christmas eve many years ago. Marcy was only five years old. She and Robin were playing tag up on the fourth floor gallery and I was down in the foyer laughing and hollering up at them. We were all having fun. Suddenly, Marcy dashed toward the stairway, Robin after her, and I kept egging her on. Well, my sweet little sister tumbled down those cursed stairs to the third floor landing, breaking her neck, like Adelaide did. I've always blamed myself for the accident. If only I had not hollered up at her to hurry, she might have been here today." Now I knew why there was no more Christmas mass at Longdon Hall. Poor little Marcy. Her ethereal likeness in the portrait hanging in the dining room had drawn me from the very first. I felt a kinship with the lovely little girl. I rose and went over to John and kissed his rugged cheek. "John," I said, "you must not torture yourself. Adelaide's death has certainly brought back painful memories, but my dear..."

John returned my kiss. "I know. I know," he answered, staring in my face, "you are a good woman, Jennifer. I sometimes wonder if I am really worthy of you." The far-away look was back in his dark eyes, and I know he was thinking of Lucille. John spoke again. "I admired Adelaide very much," he said. "Why did she have to die when there are so many nasty people taking up space in this world? Well, Robin will be free to fly now, and he probably will."

It was all I could do to keep from shouting in his face, "What about Lucille? Aren't you flying too? John must have noticed my expression, for he laid his hand gently on my shoulder and said, "You'll miss Adelaide, won't you?" I nodded, close to tears. John stared at me a while longer, then said, "Would you like to take a trip up to London for a few days?"

My heart leaped. "Oh yes, John, I would!" I answered quickly.

"Then it's all settled," returned John with a smile. "We will go next week. I have noticed how listless you have been lately, and now, with Adelaide's death preying on your mind, I'm afraid you will become ill. You need a change, Jennifer, and I'm going to see that you get it."

4

JOHN and I left for London on the following Monday. Robin and Marie had taken off somewhere the day before without so much as a farewell to anybody. They seemed in a great hurry to leave, and I suppose under the circumstances, one could not blame them. John had a talk with his mother before we left and he told me she had acted overly surprised to hear of Adelaide's death. "I told her bluntly," John said, "not to put on an act with me. And I meant it too. She clung to me, whimpering that she was only trying to block the awful event out of her mind. She said losing Marcy on that dreadful stairway was about all she could bear. She told me she was really heartbroken about Adelaide, and had cried for hours. She said she had loved Adelaide very much."

I remember remarking somewhat sarcastically to John that real love did not work in riddles. "If your mother cared that much for poor Adelaide," I said, "why in the world didn't she come downstairs and join us in our grief? She can move about. She's not that frail." The more I could put Lady Longdon down, the better I liked it. I did not mention the sharp words between Lady Longdon and Adelaide on the day of the accident; there was no use making John more miserable than he already was. I spared his feelings much more than he spared mine in those early days. John answered my question, shaking his head. "You couldn't begin to understand my mother, Jennifer. She has a cunning mind, and a way of manipulating situations to throw a sympathetic light on herself. I've seen it happen many times." I thought, *yes, John and Lucille are one of them.*

Her round face beaming, Mrs. Childs stood on the front porch waving goodbye to John and me as we rode down the drive under the tall elms to the gate, she had said to me earlier, "God bless ye dear, enjoy London with that handsome husband of yours." I promised her I would.

I was in the clouds going on this trip to London with John. He had lightly remarked to me that it was about time we had ourselves a honeymoon. Sitting beside him now, in the carriage, I gazed at his chiseled profile etched against the blue sky and thought about the child I was carrying. I decided I would tell John the happy news on our very first night in London. I was gloriously happy that day. I had pushed Lucille's filmy ghost into the back of my mind. She was just somebody who had died long ago, and I had no intention of exhuming her for the present.

Arriving in London late in the afternoon, we took a carriage to our hotel located on busy Oxford street. As we entered the regal hotel lobby, I was more than impressed with its splendor. There were potted palm trees, glittering chandeliers, and luxurious oriental carpets. Groups of people milled around, conversing in subdued tones, smiling and nodding at each other. As we checked in, a dapper bell-boy came up beside us and, picking up our luggage, told us to please follow him upstairs to the second floor. I had worn my new plum-colored satin hoop dress with a matching feathered bonnet that John had bought for me on one of his trips to Essex. I also word a small bouquet of yellow roses pinned to my waist, and if I felt like a queen on my first day in London, I had every reason to, for John, treated me like one. I felt happier that day than on the day I was married.

Our hotel was elegantly furnished with a hand-carved bed and wardrobe, a white-marble washstand, a small round table, two chairs, and dark-red carpeting underfoot. A cheery fireplace threw out rays of crackling heat. There was a deep bay window that looked down at a lively intersection. London was humming with life and so was I. It delighted me to watch the upper society glide by our window in their handsome carriages drawn by magnificent horses. Like a child at a circus, I couldn't see enough. We dined in our room on that first evening and I remember how fascinated I was watching the waiters, white towels over their arms, wheel in the dinner cart loaded with china tureen and crystal. The waiters set two places at the little round table and placed a lighted candle in the center of it; in my heart, the soft flickering flame represented my love for John. I recall how carefree and happy we were, toasting one another across the table with our glasses of fine red wine. I had John's full attention that night and it made me very happy.

Our brief stay in London is one of my tenderest memories. Each day was full and exciting, for we saw so many places of interest. I was especially drawn to the Tower of London. Its gloomy gray-stone walls and dark, eerie recesses fascinated me in a way I could not understand. As John and I passed under a spiked archway into a cobblestone courtyard, I felt as if I had been there before at another point in time. John looked down at me and laughed, "Jennifer," he said, "you are scared to death of this place, aren't you?"

I glanced at him, shaking my head. "No John, it's not that," I replied slowly, "this old tower seems vaguely familiar to me. I'm sure I've been here before."

"Jennifer, you don't believe in reincarnation rubbish, do you?" John was frowning now. Taking hold of his strong arm, I hurriedly replied, "No John, of course not." The subject was dropped, and we moved outside the gate and into our hired carriage waiting at the curb.

During our stay in London, John had showered me with expensive clothes and gifts, which I did not really want but accepted with good grace. I knew his generosity had been prompted by a guilty conscience. I once caught him looking at me with pity in this dark eyes of his and it made me angry. Lucille was back again.

Becket was at the station with the carriage when John and I stepped off the London train. He was his usual grumpy self, peering at me boldly from under his beetle eyebrows. I had only seen him once or twice since John and I were married; no doubt, the old retainer had his own views concerning my elevated station at Longdon Hall. Inside that shaggy old head of his, he probably regarded me as a low-class upstart.

The horses sped us across the wide hazy moors homeward. I was eager for the peace and quiet of Longdon Hall, after busy London. The trip had been an exhilarating change for me and I had enjoyed it, but all in all, country living was more my style; and I sighed contentedly when we finally arrived home. I had not mentioned my condition to John in London, for fear of spoiling the lovely holiday, but I had sense enough to realize I could not keep it a secret any longer. So that evening, after we had prepared for bed, I sat down in the shadow of the emerald-green lamp nervously, clutching my hands in my lap convinced that now was the time to speak out. John was busily poking the embers in the fireplace. The sound of hissing sparks filled the room.

"John, I have something important to tell you." I sat up in my chair.

John turned to me with a smile. "You have, Jennifer? Well, out with it." The glow of the hearth cast his tall shadow on the wall. I paused, then blurted out, "John, I'm going to have a baby."

John swung around again to the fire and stood with his hands behind his broad back, without a word. After an interminable time, he turned around and gazed at me, shaking his head. "Well, Jennifer, I suppose nature must have her way."

I wanted to strike out at him for taking the news so lightly. I wanted to fling Lucille in his face and say a lot of things I had on my mind, but I held it all in—there would be another time. John walked over to me and put his hand on my shoulder. "Jennifer," he said, his voice low and gentle, "you must forgive me for not carrying on like a prospective father. It's not that I don't want a child..." John paused and ran his hand through his thick black hair, fumbling for words. I could have screamed. I was so nervous. John said no more, and neither did I, so I took my hurt feelings to bed. Unable to fall asleep, I turned on my side watching John in the easy chair trying to read a book. He soon threw it aside and came to bed. I could almost hear his thoughts as he settled down on the feather mattress beside me. I longed to reach out and touch him, but we were miles apart. I knew where I stood.

The months flew by. It was now September, 1862, and our child was due about the middle of November. Though always kind and considerate, John never alluded to my condition. We went along as before; he taking care of his little trips to Sussex and his many responsibilities at Longdon Hall, and I filling in my time as best I could. I sent many hours in the kitchen with my two friends. I often look back at that time in my life and thank God for having Mrs. Childs to lean on. She was like a mother to me; she saw that I ate right and got my proper rest; I could ask her anything and get the right answer. As for Lady Longdon, well, I never saw her once in all those months. Still, that was not to say she was unaware of my condition. I knew she often stood at the gallery railing watching me go in and out of the drawing-room. I could feel her cold eyes on my back.

After taking a short stroll in the woods one afternoon, I met dear Uncle Thorne in the foyer. He looked at me and remarked slyly, "You are looking extremely well these days, my dear." And then, lowering his voice, he said, "I'm very happy for you and John... I hope it's a boy." His kind words touched my heart. Leaning down, I kissed his wrinkled cheek, whispering my thanks. "Come to the library with me, Jennifer. I've got something to give you." I floored him dutifully down the hall, admiring his springy gait and square set shoulders; though not very tall, uncle Thorne could have met a giant eye to eye. He was that kind of man. I suppose it was his inbred dignity. He had thick, well-brushed white hair that fell in a deep wave on his smooth forehead, and the bluest eyes I ever seen. In his time, uncle Thorne surely must have been popular with the ladies. How could he have helped it, having all that charm? It was always a mystery to me why he had never married.

When we entered the library, Uncle Thorne carefully closed the sliding doors behind him and told me to sit down. This room, like all the others at Longdon Hall, was strictly upper class. I had been in it only once since coming here and I remember how I ran from its walnut beamed ceiling, high arched windows, and the hundreds of leather-bound books that were neatly arranged on its three walls, Those books represented knowledge far beyond my reach. Uncle Thorne moved over to the window and opened the red-velvet drapes. A ray of yellow sunlight picked up the pattern in the oriental throw-rug at my feet; I wondered what uncle Thorne had on his mind. He came over to me, chuckling deep in his throat, "Jennifer," he began, "I am almost eighty years old, and I can still recognize a fine woman when I see one. I want you to know that I have had my eye on you since you first stepped in Longdon Hall." Uncle Thorne reached out and patted my cheek. "My dear girl," he continued warmly, "I am only trying to convey my deep admiration for you. I'm so happy you married our John. He has had more than his share of unhappiness in these last ten years. Lydia never could keep her nose out of other people's business," he observed sourly. I know he meant Lady Longdon. I waited for him to go on. "That sister-in-law of min is as healthy as I am, yet she carries on as though she might draw her last breath any minute. She's playing a wily game with John, and I think..."

I interrupted him. "I don't think John pays much attention to his mother's aches and pains, uncle Thorne. I seemed to get that impression when I heard them talking to one another. This was before John and I were married. Lady Longdon had insisted I stay in her room while she and John talked over personal matters. I felt terribly out of place."

"That's Lydia for you," exclaimed uncle Thorne, "she's never happy unless she is making somebody feel miserable." Apparently, uncle Thorne had more to tell me. After an awkward pause he continued soberly, "I realize that my brother was no angel, never-the-less, I firmly believe if he had married a less vindictive and selfish woman than Lydia, he would have been much better off today and so would Longdon Hall." He paused again and gazed up at the ceiling. It must have been very difficult for uncle Thorne to say the next few words. "Well, to make a long story short," he sighed, "John's father just walked off one day and we have not heard a word from him since. John was about ten-years-old and Robin was two at the time. John grew up despising his father, with plenty of help from Lydia and that's why he refuses to use the title, but that's foolishness. Why not use a title when you've got one?" This last made me smile. Evidently, the title was a bone of contention between John and uncle.

Uncle Thorne turned around and walked over to a small safe hidden behind an oil painting on the wall, and opening it, took out a small ancient-looking jewel box. He brought it over to me saying, "Here, Jennifer, I want you to take this box and keep it in a safe place for that little newcomer."

At first, it did not dawn on me that uncle Thorne was offering me the Queen Elizabeth jewel box that had been in the family for so long. I remember staring up at uncle Thorne absolutely tongue-tied.

"Go on! Go on! Take it!" he urged, his dear old face wreathed in smiles. Taking the box, I laid it carefully in my bloated lap; it felt very heavy. Uncle Thorne stood over us, eagerly searching my face as I lifted the lid and looked inside. Piles of emeralds, rubies, pearls, diamonds, and other precious stones stared back at me. I was holding a slice of history in my hands—it was like dream. Deeply flattered and close to tears, I thanked Uncle Thorne and told him how much I appreciated his high regard. Giving me a warm, affectionate smile, he stared down at me and said, "There's no need to thank me, my dear, and let me add this, should you ever run into any problems in the future, I'll be waiting on the sidelines to help you out." Uncle Thorne knew about Lucille. I looked away quickly. "Now, now, my dear," he said, "I did not mean to step on hallowed ground. It's just that I have your interests at heart and want you to be happy."

Keeping a firm grip on the priceless jewel box, I stood up beside the kindly old man and took his arm. I said, "I think we understand each other, uncle Thorne. I'll always be your friend and you will always be mine. No matter what happens. I want you to know that I love John with my life. It could be no other way with me." I paused and looked down in his kindly old face, "thank you for being you, uncle Thorne." He gave me a sweet smile, put his arm around my shoulder and we strolled out of the drawing-room.

I thought my confinement would never end. The long dull days at Longdon Hall dragged on through October and into November. I had lost all interest in reading and spent most of my time wandering about the grounds and the woods. Even the chilliest days did not stop me from going outside. I had to throw off my awful fear and loneliness. Dear uncle Thorne had been confined to his bed for almost a week with an acute attack of rheumatism and that did not help my state of mind either. Though thoughtful of my needs, John persisted in keeping himself on the outer rim of my life; he came and went silently, and the only time we would meet was at bedtime in our room.

As my time drew nearer and nearer, my frayed nerves were stretched to the breaking point. Then one day along about the middle of November, I went into the drawing-room and, feeling cold and miserable; I sat down in front of the fireplace clutching my woolen shawl around my swollen body. It happened to be a Saturday and, as usual, John was on one of his visits to Essex. I remember how I sat there staring into the fire wondering what was going to happen to me; would I die giving birth to this child? And if I did, would it matter at all to John? That long ago afternoon in the drawing-room at Longdon Hall is forever seared in my memory. The doctor had visited me earlier in the week, assuring me my baby would not make an appearance for at least another two weeks, but doctors don't always know everything. I can still hear the clock striking four as Mrs. Childs came into the room with my tea tray. She always knew where to find me. Setting the tray down on the table in front of me, she bent down and peered into my face. "Miss Jennifer," she said, "are you sure you are feeling all right?" I nodded my head, not saying anything. Taking my cold hands in her own, she looked down at me again and said, "Why your poor hands feel like two pieces of ice. You need some hot tea right away." Lifting the heavy silver teapot,

Mrs. Childs poured my tea, adding cream and sugar just the way I liked it, and handed it to me. "Now my girl, I am not moving one inch out of this room until you drink every drop of this," she stated, watching me closely. Forcing a smile I didn't feel, I invited her to sit down and have some tea with me. Hesitating only a second, she gingerly eased herself down on the sofa beside me.

"If Lady Longdon could see me now," she laughed, "she would have a real heart attack, wouldn't she?"

I grumbled, "Who cares about Lady Longdon?"

"Nobody, I guess, but it's her own fault for being so overbearing and nasty. I've heard she has always been that way."

"Yes, I know." I was so thankful to have Mrs. Childs with me at that moment. I did not care if the whole family trouped in and saw her sitting there.

Looking back now, I was very fortunate Mrs. Childs had lingered with me that eventful afternoon, instead of going back to the kitchen as she usually did. We sat sipping our tea, discussing one thing and another, when right out of the blue I felt my pains coming on. I stiffened out on the sofa grabbing my stomach, pains were slicing my insides like knives. I was perspiring and out of breath. "Mrs. Childs!" It all happened so fast. I was in the last stages of labor and there was no time for a doctor. I smile now when I recall how my darling son John came into the world in front of the drawing-room fireplace at Longdon Hall on November thirteenth, 1861; having been born in that unusual place somehow proved to me that my son was a true Longdon. How else could I define it?

Taking one look at me, Mrs. Childs quickly rolled up her sleeves and went to work. I can still see her strained face bending over me urging me to do this and to do that, assuring me all the while in that dear soft voice of hers not to be afraid; she would take care of me. When I heard my son's first wail, I sank back exhausted and thankful, forgetting all else. Dr. Webster told me afterwards that had he been there, he couldn't have done a better job himself. I was quietly put to bed in Mrs. Childs' care. Her loving care pulled me through the aftermath of giving birth, yet I was so depressed I'm afraid I did not care whether I lived or died. John arrived home on the following Monday and when he learned of his son's birth, he came to me immediately. He stood at the bedside staring down at me, his dark handsome face telling me nothing, then he said in a very low tone, "Thank you, Jennifer, for giving me a son." That was all! It was thought I had done him a favor. I turned my head to the wall, crying bitterly. John had already left the room.

When I finally got up and around again, I began to feel a lot better in mind and body taking care of my precious little son; he became an obsession, and I slowly began to feel whole again. John was still in my mind, of course, but not as vividly as before. I would quietly watch him go away on his weekend trips, knowing sooner or later, he would return to me and for the time being, it was enough. One day, when little John was about six months old, I took him out on the grounds in his carriage for some fresh air. His roly-poly little body started growing like a weed, and every day I discovered something delightfully different about him. He had my red-hair and John's disturbing dark eyes and when he would coo and smile at me, I would fairly burst. I loved him with the intensity of a jungle cat for its cub. He was all mine, and I always kept him close to me.

The day was balmy, sweet, and a warm sun caressed my back as I pushed little John's carriage around the side of the house. There was a wrought-iron bench under an elm tree close to the entrance to the woods. I walked over to it and sat down. I took little John out of his carriage and set him on my lap, and started playing with him. Then something made me look up at the fourth floor of the house, and there stood Lady Longdon in full view in her window, staring down at us, her lips moving as though she were muttering something to herself. She reminded me of an old black cat about to pounce on a defenseless bird. I stared up at her boldly, eye to eye, and she soon backed away from the window, letting the heavy lace curtains fall back in place.

My blood started to boil. How dare she spy on us. Not once in all those months had she asked to see her new grandchild. It was as though little John and I did not exist. I cuddled my baby son close to me, cursing Lady Longdon with all my might. I did not care if she recognized me, but for her to ignore my son was more than I could swallow. I recall how I sat there under the elm tree feeling lost and alone, and I remember too, how often I glanced at the family burial ground nearby, thinking of poor Adelaide and feeling uneasy. It was an uneasiness I could not explain.

It was late in the afternoon when I lifted little John out of his carriage and carried him up the wide front steps into the house. Mrs. Childs was standing in the hall to greet me. "Ah, there's my little man," she beamed, immediately taking him in her plump arms, "my, miss Jennifer, will you just look at that smile! It's exactly like Mr. John's, isn't it? I can see the trouble he's going to have with the ladies when he grows up." She stood chucking him under the chin and talking baby-talk to him and he gurgles back at her, happy as could be. Mrs. Childs was a genius when it came to children. She had taught me all the important things to do with children. She had taught me all the important things to do with a baby, like when he cut his first tooth and cried too much. I became frantic thinking I would surely lose him, but she just laughed and hurried down to the kitchen and came back with some concoction or other and rubbed it on little John's sore cums and he was soon happy again, and incidentally, so was I.

Mrs. Childs smiled at me, "I hope ye had a nice afternoon, Miss Jennifer. I like to get out on the grounds myself for a breath of fresh air. You sure can't find any of it in this old place," she remarked, glancing up at the stairway. "Oh, by the way, a wire came this afternoon for Mr. John." Fumbling in her apron pocket with her free hand, she took it out and gave it to me. Curious as to what the yellow envelope contained, I tucked it in my skirt belt and took little John back in my arms, telling Mrs. Childs to please bring his carriage into the house. She nodded, her soft eyes searching my face.

I said with a smile, "Now, as soon as I put little John in bed for his nap, I'll come down to the kitchen and we'll have a cup of tea."

"Ah! Miss Jennifer, I'll have it ready for you."

"Have you seen uncle Thorne today?" I asked.

"No, Miss Jennifer, I think Mr. Thorne is staying up in his room today. He does that sometimes when he is not feeling well. Poor old gent! If it were not for Mr. John and you, his life would be mighty dull around here." Mrs. Childs glanced up the stairway again. "She has always hated the sight of Mr. Thorne. I could tell you plenty about that. I'll never forget the time she quarreled with him at the dinner table. That was in the days Lady Longdon ruled the roost down here. She always dressed to the hilt for dinner and thought everybody else should too. Poor Mr. Thorne tried to calm her down being the great gentleman he was, but she wouldn't have it. She ranted and raved at him like a shrew, calling him all the nasty names she could think of. If Mr. John or Mr. Robin had been here, it wouldn't have happened." Mrs. Childs frowned, recalling her story. "I've had no use for uppity, Lady Longdon, from that day on."

I sighed and said, "Your story does not surprise me, Mrs. Childs. I feel so sorry for uncle Thorne. He's such a dear old man. How long has he lived at Longdon Hall?"

Mrs. Childs shrugged, "Oh, I would say about twenty years or so. He came here soon after Mr. John's father went away. They were twins, you know."

"Oh? I didn't know that."

"Yes," said Mrs. Childs, "and by inheritance, Mr. Thorne is the real owner of Longdon Hall and all that's in it. Of course, after his death, Mr. John will inherit everything." She smiled. "John's father was about twenty minutes younger than Mr. Thorne and he used the title, but he was not entitled to it."

Well, I had learned some more about the complex Longdon family. I wondered if little John was getting restless, so I told Mrs. Childs I would see her later, and I went upstairs to the small room that John had formerly used as an office. I had decorated the room in blue and white with lots of toys for little John to play with.

Feeling weary, I laid down on the bed and fell asleep. I awoke with a start and glanced around the room, uneasy. I rose and walked over to little John's room to see if he was all right and froze in the doorway, numb with fright. Lady Longdon was bending over little John's bed, her scrawny hands clasped around his tiny throat. I cried out, "What in the name of God are you trying to do? Get away from him!"

A cold wave of terror gripping me. I quickly dragged her away from my son's bed. She struggled like a wildcat, but I held her fast. "You miserable thing!" I fumed. "How dare you threaten my baby!"

Lady Longdon's glaring black eyes ran right through me. "Your baby!" she shouted. "What about my John? Didn't you steal him right from under my nose? But you will not have both of them. I'll see to that!" Where she got her sudden strength, I'll never know, for she squirmed out of my grasp like a frenzied animal and ran out of the room. Little John was crying. I picked him up in my arms, feeling sick to my stomach. The thought of Lady Longdon trying to choke him made me go weak in the knees and I too cried. Getting a hold of myself, I wrapped a blanket around little John and went to find Mrs. Childs. When I reached the bottom of the stairway, I glanced up at the fourth floor. Lady Longdon's door was closed. There wasn't a sound anywhere. I hurried down the hall and opened the kitchen door. I beckoned Mrs. Childs to follow me to the drawing-room. I remember the way she looked at me. She sensed something was wrong. I closed the sliding doors behind us in the drawing-room and putting my fingers to my lips, I stood listening a moment or so, then motioned her to sit down on the sofa and I sat down beside her. In a whisper, I told her what had happened upstairs. She gasped and put her hand on little John's head.

"Oh my God, Miss Jennifer, how awful! What are you going to do about it?"

I glanced at the doorway. "I don't know, but I'm going to protect little John at all costs."

"Have you told Mr. John about this?"

"No, not yet," I replied hesitantly. "John has been out on the estate since early morning."

"Well, I think you should tell him, Miss Jennifer. Do you suppose he will believe you?"

"I'm wondering about that, Mrs. Childs. I don't think I'll mention it to him just yet. But I'm so afraid Lady Longdon will get to little John again when I'm not looking. What am I going to do?" I felt helpless and terrified.

Mrs. Childs grabbed hold of my hand. "Now Miss Jennifer, you must not give way. I know exactly what to do. I've got the keys to every room in this old Hall. I'll just lock that old witch in her room so she can't get out. I know she doesn't have a key up there because I sneaked it out of her door once when she threatened to lock herself in and go on a hunger strike."

I turned and looked at Mrs. Childs. "Do you think we can get away with it?" I asked anxiously.

"Yes, I do. Mr. John only goes up there when she calls for him and if by chance she should call for him, we can explain the whole mess, and let him take it from there. It's a matter of life or death, Miss Jennifer."

I shuddered, recalling the wild look on Lady Longdon's wrinkled face when she saw me standing in the doorway of little John's room.

"Then I leave it up to you, Mrs. Childs," I sighed. "But do be careful. I'll be in my room." We rose and went out into the hall, parting at the foot of the stairs.

"I'll see you later," she whispered as she turned and walked down the hallway.

Once again, I climbed the circular stairway to our rooms on the second floor. Little John was heavy with sleep in my arms as I opened my door. The horror of the afternoon met me full force. I could still feel that horrible woman's wiry body fighting me. It was a good thing I had never been the fainting type, for who knows what might have happened to my precious baby? Sinking down in the easy chair, I leaned back and closed my eyes. This would never happen to my son again. No! Not as long as I had a breath of life in my body. I silently thanked God for Mrs. Childs' help. What would I have done without her? I could have confided in uncle Thorne. He was my friend too; however, the dear old man had himself to care for and furthermore, I did not want to upset him. I knew exactly how uncle Thorne would have reacted. He would have gone right upstairs and confronted Lady Longdon. And who knows what the outcome might have been up there in her room? No, it was wiser to keep it between Mrs. Childs and me.

Soon, there came a soft rap on my door and Mrs. Childs entered the room, her kindly face sober. She said to me in a low tone, "Don't you worry none, Miss Jennifer. I've got that one locked up tight. The only way she can escape that room is to jump out the window, and I don't think she'll attempt that."

I held out my hand to her, saying my thanks. She gave me a tender, motherly look. "I must go now," she said, "if you need me, just ring and I'll come right away." I smiled and nodded. She went out of the room.

I sat there hugging little John close to me until almost dark, then turned on the green lamp. In about a half hour, John opened the door and walked in. He came over to us and dutifully kissed little John and me on the cheek. "Here's a wire for you, John," I said, taking the yellow envelope out of my skirt belt and handing it to him.

John opened it, a frown crossed his face. "Robin and Marie are coming back home."

"When?"

"The end of next week, I guess—and I don't know whether I like it or not. Marie needs a mother's care now that Adelaide is gone." John looked at me. "Maybe you could do something about that. I'll have to mention it to Robin."

"But John, I can't..."

"The baby doesn't take up that much of your time, does he?" asked John, walking over to the washstand to wash his hands.

"No, I guess not," I replied carefully, "but truthfully, John, I just do not care for Marie. She and I would never see eye to eye."

John shrugged. "We will talk about it later."

"You look tired," I remarked, getting up and putting little John in his bed.

"I am tired. I've had a lot on my mind lately."

I gave John a sharp glance. Was it Lucille? John walked over to little John's doorway and stood with his back to me.

"Our son is gaining weight, isn't he, Jennifer?"

I felt like saying, *Oh, so you have finally noticed it*. But I didn't. I just said yes.

"Has mother asked to see him yet?" asked John, turning around to look at me.

I replied nervously, "No, not yet."

John scowled and said, "Well, in that case, she'll have to make the first move. Remember what I have just said, Jennifer, don't you weaken and take him up to her. Mother has been acting like a child ever since we were married, and I'm sick of it. I could excuse her if she was ill, but she's not ill. Dr. Webster told me she is a remarkably healthy woman for her age. Sometimes I wonder if it is senility or if it is just her nasty disposition that makes her so hard to get along with."

I listened to his words, my heart beating fast. In my opinion, Lady Longdon wasn't senile. I once had a great-aunt who became senile. She would sit in her rocking chair for hours on end smiling at everybody that came in sight. She wasn't vindictive or mean. Poor aunt Jessie wouldn't hurt a fly. John gave me a funny look. "What's the matter with you, Jennifer? Are you ill?"

I jumped nervously. "Of course not," I quickly answered. "I'm just a little tired, that's all."

John raised his thick black eyebrows. "What have you been doing all day?" I told him I had taken little John out on the grounds for an airing. "Well," he said, "I'm glad to hear that. I don't want you moping about the house all the time. You should have some friends your own age, but I guess I can't do much about that can I?" For a moment I thought John was going to bend down and kiss me, but instead of that, he walked over to the doorway saying to me, "You had better get a good nights rest. I'm going down to the library now. I have some work to do." With that, John left the room.

ROBIN AND MARIE returned to Longdon Hall the following week. I had taken little John outside for his daily airing. This time I had wheeled his carriage down to the front gate, and as soon as I was coming back along the drive under the tall canopy of elms, I heard the sound of horses behind me. I heard Marie's high-pitched voice say out loud, "Oh! Look daddy! There's Jennifer wheeling a baby carriage."

The hansom cab slowed to a stop alongside me. Robin and Marie got out. They both looked quite tan and healthy. Marie bounced over to little John's carriage and crouched down looking in his face. "Jennifer," she bubbled, "what a nice fat baby you have. I presume he's yours?"

I met her bold glance. "Yes, Marie, he's mine. Welcome home." I did not welcome her at all, in fact, I dreaded living under the same roof with her. Robin stood silently looking on. He said, "Congratulations to you and John." He glanced in the carriage. "Boy or girl?" he asked.

"A boy," I replied, "and his name is John Junior."

Robin laughed. "Well, that's proper enough. He's a carbon copy of John, all right."

Avoiding his amber eyes and the questions they were asking, I lightly opened the conversation. "You two certainly look well. May I ask where you have been?"

Marie popped up. "Daddy and I were in Paris and the south of France. Oh, it's so beautiful there. I didn't want to come back to this dumpy old place, but daddy said we must, so here we are."

Robin had sent the carriage on to the house and the three of us walked slowly up the drive. I remember the sly way Marie glanced at me, then at her father. I wondered what was going on in that mean little mind or hers. Robin was quiet. He seemed to be in a world of his own. Coming at last to the front steps, Robin paid the cab driver, then took out his luggage and set it on the ground. He took little John out of his carriage and carried him up the front steps into the house.

Marie smirked, "Now, wouldn't you think daddy was his father instead of his uncle?"

As we climbed the steps, I stared hard at her bratty little face, and she turned her head and started rattling on about the interesting places she and her father had visited in France. It was plain to see how terribly spoiled Marie was; she had on a bright-rose satin dress trimmed with black-lace flounces on the hoop skirt, and wore a close fitting black-lace bonnet on her blonde curls tied under her pert chin with a rose-satin bow. She also wore black-lace half gloves and a parasol, along with her air of supreme importance. All in all, her outfit was vulgar and flashy, and way beyond her years. It wasn't hard to imagine her dragging Robin around the Paris shops. Giving in to her every whim.

When we got to the house, I rang for Becket to bring in their luggage, and I also rang for Mrs. Childs. We stood awhile making small talk, then Robin inquired about John. I had to tell him my husband was away. Raising his eyebrows, Robin said, "On business, of course?" I nodded solemnly. "Oh well, in that case, I'll see him later, but right now I would sure appreciate a good cup of tea."

Mrs. Childs appeared just then, and I ordered tea served in the drawing-room. I caught the negative glance she gave Marie. I knew what she was thinking. We went into the drawing-room and sat down. I had taken little John in my arms, his eyelids were drooping heavily. It was time for his nap. Marie couldn't keep her hands off him. First she stroked his hair, then she tickled his chin and little John got crosser by the minute. I said briskly, "Please don't do that Marie. He's very sleepy and does not want to play just now."

She jerked her hand, giving me a stony look. "I'm not hurting him," she grumbled.

"Of course you aren't," I returned. "He'll be in a better mood after his nap. You can play with him then." Marie got up and flounced out of the drawing-room.

"Well, there she goes again," laughed Robin. "It doesn't take much to set her off. I should go after her and bring her back, but I guess I'm just too darn lazy." Robin paused for a moment, then went on, "Marie needs Adelaide's restraining hand. I've always been too easy with her." I did not offer my side of it. I did not say what a spoiled little brat Marie was and how much I disliked her, for that would have been impolite. Robin would have probably taken it as a huge joke, anyway. I began to feel uncomfortable being alone with in the great big drawing-room with Robin, however, I had no need to be concerned for he kept his eyes on little John all the while. He remarked what a fine baby he was. Mrs. Childs brought us our tea. I told her to take little John upstairs for his nap. She eyed me questionably as she took the baby in her plump arms and left the room.

"Well, Jennifer," Robin began, "my best to you and John for having such a handsome son." I could feel him staring at me in the old way. "But tell me," he said in a low tone, "are you truly happy with John?"

I stiffened. Was Robin going to start that again? Setting my teacup down on the table, I turned and met Robin squarely in the eye, replying mildly, "Of course I'm happy with John. Why do you ask me such a question?"

Grinning at me, he raised his graceful hand in protest. "No offense, I assure you, Jennifer. It's just that I want you to be happy. I will say no more."

I remember how irritated I became and how I wished Robin and his offspring had stayed in France. The mantle clock ticked loudly in my ears and a heavy silence fell between us. Robin inquired how his dear mother was doing these days. "I suppose Marie and I should go up and see her sometime this afternoon, duty, you know," he said lazily.

Suddenly, I thought of Lady Longdon being locked up in her room. I would have to get a hold of Mrs. Childs right away. I searched around in my mind for an excuse to keep Robin away from his mother for the rest of the day. "Robin," I said, "I must confess I haven't seen much of your mother lately, that is, not until this morning. You know she prefers privacy about all else and we all respect that. However, I just made it my business this morning to go upstairs and check on her. I must say, I found her in a very nasty mood. She haughtily refused the tempting break-fast tray I had prepared for her and told me to get out of her room and leave her alone. So, if I were you, I would wait until tomorrow to say hello. That would be the wisest thing to do."

Robin threw back his head, laughing at me. "Oh Jennifer, believe me, it's just not that important. I know my mother far better than you do. I won't bother with her highness today. I'm not in the mood anyway, furthermore, I doubt whether mother cares if she lays eyes on me again or not. I'm no fool. John has always been her favorite. I bet he doesn't rush up there every day to hold her hand, does he? No! I bet damn well he doesn't," declared Robin moodily, "We were once mother's puppets, Jennifer, when she pulled the string we danced. But not anymore. She ruined John's life, leaving him high and dry, and I'm not much to brag about, am I?" Robin leaned toward me slightly. I drew away from him and stood up. He stood up beside me and for a fleeting moment I felt pity for him. He looked so lost and alone. I couldn't help murmuring gently, "I'm sorry to hear that, Robin, and I'm sorry about Adelaide... and about all the other things, too."

Robin turned and gazed down at me, his arms hanging loosely at his sides. "I'm sorry too, Jennifer." I had never heard him so sober. "I am a cad in a lot of ways," he said. "Adelaide deserved a better break. Since her death, I've given it a lot of thought and I'm going to make it up to her, in my own peculiar way." He paused and stared over my shoulder. "Perhaps I can do it through Marie. Who knows?"

I didn't comment on that. Marie was a world onto herself, and unless Robin drew in the reins—which he didn't—it would be a lost cause. In a moment, Robin became his old, carefree self again. He graciously thanked me for the tea and said he was going to find Marie and take her for a stroll on the grounds. I watched him go out of the drawing-room, hunching his slim shoulders as though he were throwing off a heavy burden. From then on, I began to see Robin in a more favorable light.

After Robin left the room, I summoned Mrs. Childs and told her to go upstairs the first thing in the morning and unlock Lady Longdon's door. Mrs. Childs gave me an anxious look. "But Miss Jennifer," she frowned, "do you think it's safe to do that?"

"Oh dear, I hope so!" I replied nervously, "Robin says he won't visit his mother today, but he's going to sooner or later and he must not find her door locked. I'm going to keep my apartment door locked at all times. That woman will never lay a hand on little John again." I recall how edgy I felt saying this. "It is a good thing John is away most of the time. I wouldn't want him to suspect anything." I suddenly thought about something. "When you have been going through the hall, have you noticed Lady Longdon making any kind of fuss up there? I mean, like banging on the door or anything like that?"

Mrs. Childs looked puzzled. She replied, "Miss Jennifer, I haven't heard a peep out of her since we locked her in. I stood listening in the hall the other day for the longest time. She was as quiet as a mouse up there. Do you suppose she realizes her door is locked?"

"Of course she does." I returned, nerves on edge. "I'm sure she's tired of opening her door and she's slyly ignoring the situation. That's the part I don't understand. I would like it much better if she ranted and screamed to get out of there."

I took a deep breath and so did Mrs. Childs. I reminded her to take care of the door in the morning and report back to me. Leaning down, she gave me an impulsive kiss on the cheek.

"Now dearie, don't you fret," she said. "I'll take care of things." Her face turned sour. "I see snobby Marie has come back to live with us, eh? Well, that gives us two sly foxes to watch."

"I know exactly what you mean, Mrs. Childs. I'm afraid we will have a job on our hands watching that young lady. Robin is altogether too easy with her. He is like putty in her hands and now that her mother is gone, she will be harder than ever to handle."

"Yes indeed," nodded Mrs. Childs, "that Marie is a born trouble-maker if I ever saw one. I once caught her snooping around in one of the rooms upstairs, opening dresser drawers and the like, and when I asked her what she was looking for, she got real huffy and ordered me back downstairs where I belonged. Miss Jennifer, I swear if Marie hadn't been a Longdon, I would have smacked her sassy face!" Mrs. Childs' round face was grim when she finished speaking. It was plain to be seen that Marie was going to be a thorn in both our sides. I glanced at Mrs. Childs and said, "Do you think we can keep her in line?"

"Yes, I sure do," she replied. I grabbed hold of her warm, plump hand. No more needed to be said. We understood one another perfectly. When I look back on those early years at Longdon Hall, I thank God for having found a friend like Sarah Childs. She gave me strength and courage many times over. I grew to love her very much.

The summer of 1862 was uneventful. Robin and Marie remained in their rooms on the third floor, seldom appearing downstairs except for dinner each evening. Marie, oddly enough, was on her good behavior. She would sit quietly at the table, not interrupting the conversation as before. I wondered if Robin had been successful in toning her down. Now and then I would catch Robin eyeing me across the table, a sad half-smile on his handsome blonde face, and I would smile back at him in a friendly way. Dear uncle Thorne, bless his heart, still blustered his way through the evening meal, arguing a point in his own inimitable way, winking an eye at me all the while.

My life with John had become dull and meaningless. I loved my husband and stood in awe of him, and he was kindness itself to me. He often remarked how proud he was having a song to carry on the Longdon name, yet not once since we were married had he told me he loved me. When we were alone together, he was so withdrawn I felt as though I was on another planet. I knew his thoughts were with Lucille and how I envied her. The woman haunted me day and night. I had nightmares of a tall willowy creature with blazing eyes choking the life out of me and I would wake up in a cold sweat.

One day in September, I was sitting in the drawing-room working on a piece of needlework. I had put little John to bed for his nap with my door locked tight against the possibility of Lady Longdon visiting the second floor. I needn't worry though, for Mrs. Childs informed me she had been as docile as a kitten since Robin and Marie returned to Longdon Hall. She spent most of her time in bed complaining of severe heart pains and numerous other ailments, playing it to the hilt. My friend also told me that Marie visited her grandmother quite often. "And would you believe it Jennifer," Mrs. Childs commented, "that sassy little imp actually spends hours up there holding Lady Longdon's hand. I know perfectly well they despise one another. I can see it in their eyes." I recall my surprise hearing this. I remarked that *birds of a feather usually flock together* and Mrs. Childs agreed with me.

As I sat absorbed in my needlework that long-ago afternoon, I heard somebody open the drawing-room door. I turned around to see who it was. Very dapper in a light-tan suit and white-ruffled shirt, Robin crossed the room and sat down beside me on the sofa. I was surprised to see him. "Hello Robin," I said, dropping my needlework in my lap.

"Hello Jennifer," he returned, smiling. Something in his amber eyes bothered me.

"How's Marie?" I asked lightly. "We don't see much of her these days. Why do you keep yourselves cooped up all the time? Are you afraid of us?"

"Of course not," he said. "I thought perhaps if I kept Marie close to me at all times, I might be able to break her nasty ways. I think I have made some progress." Robin folded his arms across his chest and sighed. I told him I noticed an improvement in Marie's table manners, that she seemed quieter and less talkative.

"Good," said Robin. "I'm glad you have noticed some change in her. Now I can say what's on my mind."

I glanced at him, wondering what he meant.

"Jennifer," he resumed soberly, "I've decided to go to America and join the Confederate army. I've been reading a lot about the war over there and my sympathies lie with the South. Believe me, I'm strictly against slavery and all it implies. However, I do respect the Confederate's rights to keep on governing them-selves. Abolition is all well and good, and I'm sure Mr. Lincoln and his cabinet members consider it their God given duty to free the Negroes, but let me tell you Jennifer, the South is not going to give up easily. The issues go too deep."

Robin's serious words alarmed me. I had heard there was a civil war going on in America and it could have been taking place on the moon for all us British people cared. Hadn't we stopped worrying about the colonies since 1776? I studied Robin's profile. It was very hard for me to understand his motive. "Robin," I began gently, "I don't know what to say... are you sure you want to do this? What about Marie?"

His face a complete blank, Robin rose and walked over to the fireplace and stood a while with this back to me, then he turned around and stared at me. "I don't know how to put this Jennifer," there was a long pause, "will you look after Marie while I'm gone? I know I should not expect it of you... perhaps I have to prove something to myself with this war thing."

I had known all along that Robin was deeply disturbed about something, and it wasn't me. He was wrestling with himself, but why on earth did he choose to fight somebody else's war? It did not make sense.

"Robin, of course, we'll look after Marie," I calmly replied, not in the least enthusiastic about the job. I gazed at him standing slender as a reed, one elbow draped nonchalantly on the mantelpiece and I suddenly went cold. "Robin," I said, "why don't you think this over? Don't you realize you might... be killed over there?"

Leveling me with narrowed eyes, Robin responded very slowly, "Yes Jennifer, I've thought about that possibility. Would it matter to you if I were killed?" This last was barely a whisper.

I looked away, replying briskly, "You know perfectly well neither John nor I would want to see anything like that happening to you. Oh! Robin, do change your mind and stay at home where you belong... for the life of me, I can't understand why you want to sacrifice yourself for a cause that has nothing whatever to do with us!"

I remember the deadly serious answer I got from Robin. "Jennifer," he said, "I don't expect you to understand... it's just something between me and myself, that's all."

Gathering up my needlework, I got up from the sofa, ready to go up and see if little John was awake. "When do you plan on sailing to America?" I asked.

"Probably in about a week or two." Robin gazed down at his well-polished shoes.

I clutched my needlework and frowned. "Oh, I see. Well, I must leave you. Little John will be awake by now." With that, I hurried out of the drawing-room in a muddled state of mind.

❦

True to his work, Robin left for America the following week. I expected Marie to carry on in a big way, but she said very little when we gathered in the drawing-room to say goodbye to Robin.

Besides Marie, there was uncle Thorne, John, Mrs. Childs and myself. John was furious with Robin for getting himself involved in the American war. Earlier in the week he had pleaded with his brother to drop the idea and remain at home, reminding him sharply that his foremost duty was to his young daughter and not to some far off political mess over which he had no control. I had overheard part of the heated conversation one day as I passed by the drawing-room and I can still hear Robin's flat reply that his mind was made up and that was it.

I remember Marie strolling over to the rain-streaked bay window to gaze out and Robin close on her heels, whispering something in her ear. She threw her arms around his neck sobbing, "Oh Daddy!" It was a tense moment as Robin walked back and shook hand with each one of us. We wished him well, and he promised to keep us posted as to his whereabouts. Then he walked silently out of the room.

It was now Christmastime and Robin had been gone three months. He wrote to us that he was stationed in a remote part of South Carolina. He said southerners were fighting like tigers and it looked as though they held the winning hand, driving the Yankees back on all fronts.

John pulled a sour face as he read Robin's letter. "The young fool!" he scowled. "I wonder what he is trying to prove?"

I knew that John, deep down, worried about Robin. Often in his sleep at night, I would hear him mumble, *Watch out, Robin! Watch out!*

The big hall was as silent as a tomb that Christmas eve. Mrs. Childs and Mrs. Bevins and all the other servants were in the kitchen busily preparing a huge turkey, mince pies, plum pudding, and all the trimmings for the next day. I had not seen

Marie all day. She had kept to herself a lot since her father left Longdon Hall and I was thankful for that. I saw to it that her clothes were kept in good order and had hired a private tutor for her. Marie's schooling had been somewhat spotty, but nevertheless she was a bright intelligent child and she soon mastered her lessons, with tongue in cheek, I might add. I was afraid at first that she would put up a fuss with her new teacher, but she coasted right along not seeming to care one way or the other. Sly Marie.

I remember I was in the drawing room that Christmas eve arranging a garland of mistletoe across the mantelpiece. John was upstairs working on some papers. When a piercing scream rang out in the rotunda. I rushed out of the room and up the stairs to Marie, who stood transfixed on the third floor landing.

"For heaven's sake, Marie, what's wrong?" I cried.

"Oh Jennifer," she blubbered, shaking like a leaf. "I've just seen my mother! I was coming down the stairs from grandma's room and there she stood, right where you are standing now. She stared at me out of two black holes where her eyes should have been. Oh Jennifer! I am so scared!"

I glanced up at the fourth floor; Lady Longdon's door was closed, and John was on his way up the stairs from the second floor.

"What's the trouble in here?" he asked, eyeing us sternly. I told him what happened. He turned to Marie and said, "Young lady, that's a lot of rubbish. I don't want to hear anymore of it, do you hear? There are no such things as ghosts. There never was and there never will be."

Marie scowled at John, then ran around the third floor gallery to her room, slamming the door behind her. "Utterly ridiculous!" scoffed John as he went on down the stairs, me following. I wanted to say a lot of things, but I didn't.

I returned to the drawing-room and went on with my job, thinking of poor Adelaide. Did Marie really see her mother on the landing, or was it only her imagination? I felt a chill run through me. I glanced up at the clock. It was almost 10 p.m. I finished putting up a few more Christmas decorations in the drawing-room, then I poked the hearth, extinguished the lamps and went upstairs to bed. I suppose it was somewhere around 3 a.m. when I awoke to a dull scraping and moaning sound outside our bedroom door. I got out of bed, lighted a candle, and crept over to the door, and opened it. Holding the candle up high, I carefully searched to gallery; nobody was there. I walked over to the railing and glanced up at the upper galleries and all was dark and silent. Going back in our room, I locked myself in and stood with my back to the door wondering about the strange sounds. Suddenly, Lady Longdon flashed in my mind. Would she be wandering about the galleries at this hour in the morning? I did not think so, for Mrs. Childs had mentioned once that the woman took a sleeping pill every night at bedtime. I stood there for a while thinking about this and that, when to my horror the same scraping sound came on the door panel close to my ear and I almost dropped the candle on the floor. John's sleepy voice called out across the room; "For God's sake, Jennifer, what are you doing standing there for?" I did not answer him but blew out the candle and hurried back to bed, shivering with fright and the cold.

❧ 6 ❧

JOHN'S ABSENCES from Longdon Hall became more prolonged. Sometimes a week would pass before I laid eyes on him, and I did not like it. He always returned home preoccupied, paying little attention to me. Once, I questioned his staying away for so long and got nowhere. John quietly explained that he had pressing business matters to take care of and I shouldn't go on about it.

I recall that heartbreaking day soon after the new year, when John returned home unexpectedly, I was down in bed with a severe cold, feeling sick, and miserable. Though more than happy to see him, I could not restrain my irritation when he appeared in the bedroom doorway. I began acidly, "Well, John, I sometimes wonder if you live here anymore. I can take your neglect, but our baby can't. He doesn't deserve it."

I'll never forget the look on John's face when I said that. He approached the bed lashing out at me. "I don't want to hear anymore of this, do you understand?" he glared down at me angrily. "My son is the only reason I come back here. It's not because I find you particularly alluring." It's about time you know I only married you to spite my mother and to spawn a son to carry on the Longdon name. And furthermore, I've been seeing the one and only woman in my life. I've been in love with her for years and now she is dying and I intend to stay with her to the end." Walking over to his desk, John scribbled something down on a slip of paper. He looked up at me and said, "If you need me in case of an emergency, you can reach me at this address." He walked out of the bedroom.

Stunned at what I had just heard, I sat up on the side of the bed and started to cry. Our marriage was a farce right from the beginning, and I had wasted my time waiting for John to tire of Lucille and come rushing back into my arms. Pride and anger took hold of me. John Longdon had made a fool of me. I was of no consequence at Longdon Hall except that I was little John's mother. Dragging myself into my clothes, I went downstairs to find Mrs. Childs. On my way down, I heard Marie skulking around the second-floor gallery. I wondered what she was up to but I did not look up to find out. Reaching the foot of the stairs, I hesitated, then went on down the hall to the kitchen and asked Mrs. Bevins where Mrs. Childs was. She told me she had gone up to Lady Longdon's room, so I told her to please send her to me in the drawing-room when she got back.

Entering the drawing-room, I flopped down on the sofa in front of the fire. I felt weak, feverish, and ached all over. John and Lucille drifted in and out of my mind like a nasty dream. All of a sudden, everything turned black, and I fainted dead away. I don't know how long I lay there, but when I came to, I saw Mrs. Childs' broad face anxiously bending over me.

"Miss Jennifer! Miss Jennifer! Are you ill?" she cried, slapping my hands. Giving me a steady look, she placed the back of her soft hand on my forehead and immediately helped me up from the sofa and up the winding stairs to my bed where I spent three solids weeks battling pneumonia. On the tenth day after the crises, Mrs. Childs told me my temperature had reached the danger point. She said that I became delirious and kept calling for John to come back home also that I muttered *Lucille* over and over again.

I recall how the sun streamed in the bedroom window that morning, lighting up the red-ruby carpet. I was feeling much better, but still very weak. Mrs. Childs was perched on the side of the bed, feeding me a bowl of hot broth. I knew she had more to say to me. She waited until I had finished the broth. "Miss Jennifer," she began evenly, "where in the world is Mr. John? I was at my wit's end trying to find him when Dr. Webster told me you might die." Her thick brown eyebrows came together in a frown. "I questioned Mr. Thorne and Lady Longdon. Neither one knew where he was, and when I told Lady Longdon how terribly ill you were, she brushed it off as nothing, declaring she had her own health to think about. She said she needed Mr. John much more than you did. I was so mad at that old woman I almost slammed the door off its hinges when I left the room!"

I smiled weakly at my dear friend and took hold of her hand. What would I have done without her? I told her all about John and Lucille and when I finished my story she stood gazing down at me, a deep softness in her eyes. "My, my," she sighed, "I never would have thought if of Mr. John. You poor dear. No wonder you are down sick, but don't worry, my love, you still have Sara Childs to lean on! Yes, sir! And this will be our secret. I'll never open my sough to other about this." She thought for a moment. "Do you suppose Mr. Thorne suspects anything?"

I had wondered about that too. I knew the dear old soul's eyes and ears missed nothing that went on in that house and I longed to confide in him also, but could not bring myself to mention John's name when uncle Thorne visited me later on that afternoon. I answered Mrs. Childs' question. "I wouldn't be surprised if Mr. Thorne did know about this — even though he's in his eighties, his mind is razor sharp, and he observes people, tongue in cheek, he wouldn't cause trouble for anybody. He's too much of a gentleman for that."

"Ah yes! That's the very word for him, Miss Jennifer. Mr. Thorne blusters once in a while to keep the others in line, but I've never known him to be downright mean to anybody. All of us servants adore Mr. Thorne and would do anything for him." Smiling sweetly, she gently pushed me back on my pillows saying, "That's quite enough talking for now, my girl. I'll look in on you later after I've seen to little John." She leaned down and kissed my cheek.

"Oh dear, little John isn't sick too, is he?" I mumbled.

"No, no, love, of course he's not sick. That youngster of yours is as strong as a week. I've kept the lad close to me since you have been ill." I guess she must have read my panicky thoughts.

"Now Miss Jennifer," she soothed, "I don't want you to fret your pretty head about the old lady getting to him again. Nellie stands guard in my room when I'm seeing to things and it's working out fine."

I was relieved to hear that. I trusted our little maid, Nellie. Settling deeper into my pillows, I closed my eyes and heard the door click behind Mrs. Childs as she left the room. I could see that slip of paper on John's desk and was glad nobody found it. I did not care whether I ever saw John again or not. I dozed for a while and woke again feeling weak and washed out, my body soaked with perspiration. The awful fever was gone. I know that I was now on the mend, but my heart wasn't. Had John slapped my face, or even if he had knocked me down, I'm sure I could have stood it, but not his cruel words. They were red-hot coals in my mind, yet I had to deal with it somehow.

A timid rap came at the door. It slowly opened and there stood uncle Thorne framed in the doorway, smiling at me. I nodded and smiled back. He closed the door and took a chair beside my bed. "Are you feeling any better, my dear?" he asked, his anxious blue eyes searching my face.

"Oh yes, I'm feeling much better, though I'm still awfully weak."

"Yes, yes, indeed. I know how pneumonia weakens one. I've had several bouts of it myself." "I might be just an old man, but that doesn't say I'm not smart enough to see how the wind is blowing with my nephew John." I turned my head away. "Jennifer, do you know where John is?" he asked gently. I turned around and looked at him; my eyes wet with tears. "There now, there now," he sighed. "I can see that you do, and so do I. I've suspected all along that John was visiting Lucille Merridith, you see? I know a lot more than you think I do."

The dam burst and words tumbled out of my mouth one by one. I told uncle Thorne everything. I told him John had left me and I did not know how to handle it.

Uncle Thorne wagged his shaggy head from side to side, frowning darkly. "John Longdon deserves a good tongue lashing for this and he'll get one when I see him. I don't like to see you cry, little Jennifer. It's callous of John causing you such grief and all because of a broken romance which should have died out years ago." A far-away look came in his eyes, "I can't say Lucille wasn't a nice girl, I remember her very well and would have welcomed her into the family, however, my determined sister-in-law had other ideas about the match and lost no time breaking them up."

"Yes... so, I have heard." I sighed wearily. Uncle Thorne rose and stood gazing down at me in the saddest way. "My dear young lady," he added kindly, "please allow me to apologize for John and remember, I'll prop you up under any circumstances. It's just about time somebody around here took a firm stand. I'm still the head of this household, whether the others think so or not, and I intend to exert my authority."

I took hold of his hand and squeezed it. "Thank you, uncle Thorne. I love you very much. I won't forget what you have just said to me. I might certainly need your help before this thing between John and me is resolved."

Uncle Thorne leaned down and brushed a kiss on my forehead. "I'm happy to see you feeling better, my dear. I'll leave you now so you can rest." With that, he turned and slowly went out of the room.

Day by day, I regained my strength and in no time—thanks to Mrs. Childs' loving care—was my old self again, and believe it or not, thought less and less of John and Lucille. For little John took up all of my time and thought. One afternoon, about a month after my illness, I told Becket to bring the carriage around to the front door. Bundling little John in his warm blankets, I carried him downstairs, eager to get outside in the fresh air. As I passed the drawing-room doorway, Marie suddenly darted out in front of me, scaring me half to death. "Oh Jennifer! I am so sorry," she cried. "I didn't know you were out here." She gave me a keen glance. "Say, how are you anyway? Aren't you pretty weak after that awful pneumonia?"

I assured her I did not feel weak and was taking little John out for a carriage ride.

"Oh! May I please come too?" she coaxed, giving me a syrupy smile. I dread that, yet I could not refuse her, so I told her to hurry into her things and she could come along.

The day was sunny and cheerful, though chilly. Marie settled back beside me on the carriage seat, her hands folded demurely in her lap. Now and then she glanced down at little John's face, her thoughts elsewhere. Suddenly, Marie began talking about her father and how much she needed him. "Do you suppose my daddy will be killed, Jennifer?" she asked soberly. This kind of shook me up. I had almost forgotten that Robin was fighting a war.

"Don't think of such a thing, Marie," I remonstrated sharply. "You must believe that you will see your father again."

Marie gave a glum look. "Wouldn't you be afraid too, if you were me? My father is thousands of miles away fighting a silly war and here I sit with neither a mother nor a father to lean on. Thank heavens I've got a grandmother to talk to." Marie turned and peered hard into my face. "Grandmother told me a lot of things about uncle John. She said he was madly in love with a very beautiful girl, but grandma didn't think it was acceptable and she told her so, just like that." Marie snapped her fingers. "How grandma laughed when she told me this and I did too. It must have been funny to see, because she said the girl and uncle John faced up to her boldly and there was a bitter argument between uncle and grandmother. The girl got so upset she never set foot in Longdon Hall again. Uncle John treated grandmother very mean after that. I'm glad that girl was put in her place. I would have to. We don't want trash worming their way into the Longdon family, do we, Jennifer?"

Marie's double-barreled remark left me cold; I did not rise to the bait, but began talking about little John and the weather. We rode to the far side of the estate and across a broad ravine, muddy water splashing high up on the carriage wheels. Then Becket took a shortcut home again. I gazed at Marie's tense, cameo-like profile; I could see that she was cold. "Marie," I said, "why didn't you wear a warmer coat today? You are turning quite blue with the cold."

Marie flounced around on the seat and glared at me. "I'm not a bit cold," she exploded passionately. "I'm furious and disgusted!

Why doesn't my father come back home where he belongs? Damn, damn that idiot war!"

"Why Marie!" I gasped, "I'm surprised at you. I forbid you to use such language."

"Jennifer Longdon, you can't forbid me to do a thing, and don't try to either!" cried Marie, thrusting out a belligerent chin.

Thank heaven we had turned in at the gate to Longdon Hall. Marie's insolence was getting to me in a way I did not like. When we drew up at last in front of the house, I got out of the carriage and hurried up the steps, Marie lagging behind me.

One night about a week later, I turned out my beside lamp and settled down to get some sleep. Little John was cutting teeth, and he had literally worn me out all evening with his fussy crying. Almost drifting off. I suddenly lifted my head and listened to a moaning sound out in the gallery. It was slowly approaching my room, getting louder and louder. I got out of bed, lighted a candle, and opened my bedroom door, and peered out into the dark gallery. As I stood there, I heard three distinct raps coming from the top of the stairway, and the moaning sounds started again. Suddenly, Adelaide flashed in my mind. I braced myself, fearing the worst. Holding the candle aloft, I bravely moved toward the stairway, my heart in my throat, then I heard a snicker close by and my candle reflected Marie's bold face staring up at me. She was seated on the top step, laughing for all she was worth.

Well, that was it! I had finally reached the end of my rope with Miss Marie. My face hot with rage, I dragged her up to her feet and slapped her face. She squealed and tried to break away from me, but I held her fast. "What do you think you are doing out here?" I demanded hotly. I was so mad at her I could have slapped her again just for good measure.

Marie hissed in my face. "I'm going to tell my grandmother what you just did to me! She'll fix you for this! And you had better keep your cruddy hands off me from now on, or I'll shove you down the stairs when you're not looking!" She glared hatefully at me in the candlelight and for a second I thought she was going to carry out her threat right there and then. However, I was in command and she knew it.

"Go to your room," I ordered sharply. "And don't ever let me catch you trying a stunt like this again... and furthermore, I don't care what you tell your grandmother. You can tell her for me that I will be available anytime she wishes to discuss this matter. Now you just turn around and go up those stairs to your room!" Marie gave me a black look as she slowly climbed the stairs to the third floor gallery. I followed close on her heels, making sure she obeyed me. Half way around the gallery she swung around and stuck out her tongue at me, then darted into her bedroom, slamming the door behind her. Shaking with anger, I stood listening. The rotunda was as quiet as a tomb; I hurried downstairs to my room and shut the door.

Surprisingly enough, I did not hear a word from Lady Longdon the next day or anytime thereafter, and I did not worry about it. By now, I was standing on my own two feet in the Longdon household. I was not about to be intimidated by anyone, much less Marie. Since John's departure, I had done some heavy thinking. I was bound and determined to stand my ground. Both little John and I were entitled to our rights and I would fight back just as hard as I knew how, if Lady Longdon dared to oppose us. As for Marie, well time would tell.

❦

The winter of 1863 was unusually cold and blustery. I was forced to stay indoors where it was warm, whether I wanted to or not. I spent my time sewing in my room, little John playing on the floor at my side. I remember looking down at his innocent baby-face, feeling very bitter and alone. I'd had no word from John all winter, though Mrs. Childs informed me John had written her a couple of times regarding household matters. She said he did not mention little John or me. Having had another attack of rheumatism, uncle Thorne had not come down to dinner in the last few weeks, and I missed him. Marie ate upstairs with her grandmother, so that left me alone at the huge dining table with only my dull thoughts for company.

One dismal afternoon in early March, I took little John and a basket of needlework down to the drawing-room. Becket had built a roaring fire in the hearth. Its comforting warmth met us at the door. The magnificent old room opened its arms like an old friend. I set little John down on the white-fur rug in front of the fireplace and gave him his toys to play with. Now sixteen months old, he was eager to explore every nook and cranny he came across. A wary eye on my son, I sat down on the sofa and spread a new piece of needlework across lap. It was a coverlet for little John's bed. I studied the intricate pattern, hoping I wouldn't have a job ahead of me. Then Robin came into my mind. We had only gotten one letter from him since he went to war—somehow; I wanted to reach out and tell him to come home at once, that we needed him. I threaded my embroidery needle and began to sew. Unnoticed, my cunning little son had toddled over to the other side of the drawing-room on a tour of his own. I jumped up and got to him just in time to snatch a priceless knick-knack out of his chubby little fists. Swooping him up in my arms, I carried him back to the fur rug and told him to stay right there. The look he gave me was totally John's. He soon became interested in one of his toys, so I settled down again with my sewing.

Lively orange flames danced around the logs in the fireplace, and a peaceful feeling engulfed me. I suddenly felt as light and free as a feather. It was as though I had been freed from some dark prison into the sunlight again. The feeling was hard to analyse, for I certainly had enough on my dish these days without daydreaming. Suddenly, I heard Marie's voice behind me. "What are you making, Jennifer?" she asked timidly. I turned at once and looked up at her. I did not know she had come into the room. Why did Marie sneak up on people? She came around and slid down beside me on the sofa with a sad look on her dove-like face. Was she playing tricks again? I wondered. She gazed down at my sewing and I showed her what I was doing.

"Oh, that's darling!" she exclaimed. "Would you show me how to embroider sometime, Jennifer?" I said I would. I immediately sensed something different about the child as she bent over my sewing. There was an air of humbleness in her smile. What did that mean? I soon found out.

Marie got up from the sofa and knelt down on the fur rug with little John. She flung her arms around his neck and kissed him. Great tears rolled down her cheeks when she finally looked up at me. "Oh Jennifer," she choked, "I'm sorry I was so nasty to you. I guess I'm not worth much, am I? Oh dear. I have been so lost and alone since daddy went away that I just wanted to... kill... myself... and not be in the way anymore." Marie dropped her face in her hands and sobbed as though her heart would break. I was stunned and touched. I got up and pulled the child up in my arms and told her it was all right. "Oh Jennifer," she sobbed, "even my own grandmother told me to get out of her sight. She chased me down the stairs with her cane and I thought she was going to hit me with it." Marie's hot tears stained the bodice of my lavender dress. She trembled like a leaf in my arms and I felt deep pity for the lonely little girl. Taking out my handkerchief, I dabbed her lovely amber eyes, murmuring softly, "Now listen, Marie, you must stop torturing yourself. I forgive you. You and I are going to be good pals from now on, you'll see. I promised your father I would take care of you and I intend to do that." I tilted her chin and peered into her tear-stained face. "Now, shall we forget what has happened and start all over again? Just you and me?" Marie nodded her golden curls vigorously. "Very well then," I said, "now wash your face and come back down here. I will have Mrs. Childs bring us our supper in here. Would you like that?"

Marie's face lit up like the sun. "Oh Jennifer. I'd adore it." I watched her skip out the door, and I smiled.

❧ 7 ❧

THE MONTHS ROLLED BY. Marie had been my shadow, and I learned to love her as my own. She was wonderful with little John. She would take him for long walks around the grounds, weather permitting, and watched over him whenever I had other things to do around the house. Once, she said to me, "Jennifer, do you really like me?" I remember taking her by the shoulders and looking deeply into those yellow eyes of hers.

"Of course I do," I replied. "I've grown to love you very much, Marie. I don't know what I'd do without you."

Marie's eyes widened. "Then I really mean that much to you, Jennifer?"

"Yes, you really do. Now run along and play."

One day, while looking out the drawing-room window, I saw a cab pull up at the door. A messenger boy ran up the steps holding a letter. In a few minutes, Mrs. Childs came in and handed it to me. It was from John and it read: *Dear Jennifer, Lucille passed away at six o'clock this morning. I shall never return to Longdon Hall. I hope you understand and will forgive me for all the hurt I've caused you and little John. This is something beyond all of us. John.*

I crumpled the letter in a ball and threw it on the floor. Mrs. Childs went over and picked it up and read it. "Oh my dear," she moaned. "I am so sorry."

"Well, I'm not." I returned briskly. "I'm glad John's not coming back. We don't need him." And I meant it. My love for John Longdon had faded into thin air and I have become a brand new person. I was not the silly little ninny he had married. I smile and patted Mrs. Childs plump back. She smiled back at me.

"What are you gong to do, Miss Jennifer?" she asked timidly.

"I'm going to hold the fort," I laughed. I felt secure, for I knew at last just where I stood. John had been gone for over six months and I had grown used to it. A weight had been lifted off my back.

w

On New Year's day, I took Marie and little John for a drive on the moor. Becket had taught me how to handle the horses. They were handsome, docile creatures, therefore, I had little fear they would run off with us. The air was brisk and clean in our lungs as we rolled onto the wide, smooth moor. All of us had woolen scarves wound around the lower part of our faces against the sharp wind, also a cozy fur-lined robe spread across our laps. After a few turns around the moor, we rode back home, happy and carefree. I remember little John tugging away at his scarf and Marie pulling it back up on his face, scolding him all the while. As we neared the gate, I noticed a carriage turn onto the road and drive east of Longdon Hall. I was curious about it.

As soon as we got into our warm drawing-room, I rang for tea. The three of us joined hands and greeted the New Year, singing songs. Little John lisped his words in such a cut way, Marie and I couldn't resist hugging him. When Mrs. Childs brought our tea and cakes, I noticed how quiet she was. She gave me a strange look as she left the room, and it bothered me. We soon finished our snack and Marie got down onto the floor to play with little John. I picked up my sewing. A thumping sound started down the hallway in our direction. Suddenly there stood Robin framed in the doorway, leaning on a crutch. His eyes were two burned holes in his grim face and he was thin. Worst of of all, he had lost a leg. I couldn't believe what I saw.

Marie jumped up and rushed over to him screaming, "Daddy! Daddy!" flinging her skinny arms tightly around his neck as though she would never let go.

"Baby, baby, it's all right," Robin murmured huskily. He brushed his eyes with the back of his hand. Finally, Marie led him across the room to me. I was speechless with shock. "Hello, Jennifer," he said. He propped his crutch up against a chair nearby and eased himself down on the seat. I saw him wince, lifting the stump of his leg in a more comfortable position. Marie was glued to her father's chair, her arm around his shoulder.

I mumbled, "Welcome home, Robin." There was so much more I wanted to say, but the words stuck in my throat.

Robin stared at me dully. "I suppose I should have notified you," he sighed, staring off into space.

I could not keep my eyes off his poor leg. It was incredible that this pitiful, war-weary man sitting across from me was Robin Longdon. I felt terribly sorry for him. He told me at last that most of his company had been wiped out in some battle or other. I could tell it pained him to talk about it. "By the grace of God," he continued in a thin tone. "I escaped with just this." He motioned to his leg. I didn't want to hear any more. It was enough that Robin had returned to us. I remember the wind howling around the tall windows, and Robin's gaunt face staring at me in the fireplace's shadow. A mournful silence fell over us, then Marie spoke. "Daddy, Jennifer and I are going to make you forget that nasty old war. We're going to love you and make you all well again. Aren't we Jennifer?" Marie's eyes pleaded with me over the top of her father's head.

"Of course we are," I quickly answered. I went over and laid my hand on Robin's arm and said, "Don't you think you should rest awhile? Do you want us to help you upstairs?"

Robin jerked up his head defensively. "No! No! That won't be necessary. I can make it on my own." I had blundered. Robin would never lean on anybody again. Marie proudly escorted her father to the drawing-room door. I heard him say, "No baby, that is far enough." Patting her head, he limped away. Marie was crying bitterly when she came and sat down beside me on the sofa. I put my arms around her and cried, too. War did horrible things to men.

As time passed, Robin slowly adjusted to being home again. He began to take an interest in things and he was not so tense, though certainly the war had left its grim mark on him. For a long while, he did not inquire about John, yet I would often catch him staring at me and I knew what was going through his mind. For the most part, Robin stayed upstairs in his room and Marie waited on him hand and foot. She couldn't do enough for her father and I'm sure her loving care helped restore his state of mind. It took time, of course. Uncle Thorne remarked how happy he was having Robin home again. The dear old man's eyes filled with tears as he said to me, "Jennifer, that boy deserves a medal for what he has been through. I never thought he had it in him. I've called him an egotistical fool and other things in my time, but I've got to admit he has proved himself a true Longdon. Robin did not have to go and fight in that senseless war, but he did and lost a leg in the bargain. It takes a lot to prove oneself that way." I remember telling uncle Thorne that I felt exactly the same way about

Robin. And now that we had him home again, we must take good care of him.

One day in late summer. I had just come indoors after a stroll in the garden and was arranging some roses in a crystal vase on the hall table when I looked up and saw Robin slowly descending the stairs, his face dark with anger. He hesitated on the bottom step and adjusted his crutch. I went over to him and said hello.

Robin looked through me. "I've just been upstairs talking to my mother." His tone was rough. "And all I've heard for the last hour is, '*Where is my John? Where is my John?*' And I am sick of it." Robin pointed at his injured leg. "Do you know what my sainted mother said about this? She told me I should have lost both of my legs for sticking my nose in a war that didn't concern me! I actually believe that woman enjoys see me a cripple!"

I wanted to reach out and touch Robin. I felt something deep inside of me rebelling against all the hurt he had suffered and besides; I wanted to rush up those stairs and shout at that old woman as she never had never been shouted at before, but it would have done no good. I invited Robin into the drawing-room for a while and he nodded his head. As we seated ourselves on the sofa, he immediately brought up Adelaide's tragic death. I was surprised he wanted to discuss the subject. Robin's handsome face worked painfully as he said to me, "You know, Jennifer, I really did love Adelaide. I realize it now that she's gone and I know I gave her a difficult time. Was it because I needed something she couldn't give me, or was it just my overblown vanity? I'll never know for sure, will I?"

I turned and faced him. "Robin," I said gently. A strange tug at my heart. "It's best to let bygones be bygones. Adelaide would tell you so if she were here. I'm sure she has forgiven you wherever she is, so don't dwell on it anymore."

Robin ran his slender hand through his rich blond hair, and we were quiet for a while. Then suddenly he asked if I had heard from John. I wasn't afraid of the question. I knew Robin meant well, so I explained that John had left me for good after Lucille had died and that I hadn't the faintest idea where his brother was or what he was doing. Leaning back on the sofa, Robin stated up at a scenic oil painting above the mantelpiece. "I'm not the least surprised," he said at last. "I hate to say this, Jennifer, but that love affair had been going on for years. But I doubt had they married that they would have made a go of it with my mother on the scene." Robin turned and looked at me. "Too bad my brother had to mess up your life."

I dropped my eyes and started twisting my wedding ring around my finger. I could feel Robin's eyes boring through me. I was relieved he didn't say anymore about John. Words were meaningless anyway.

❧

Two years passed. Little John had grown into an intelligent husky five-year-old and we were so proud of him. I had engaged a tutor for him. A Mr. Ronald Price, who was about twenty years old and proficient in the art of teaching. The young man came every day from 10 am until 2 pm. Little John eagerly awaited him.

Robin had taken over the responsibilities of the Hall and consulted uncle Thorne whenever improvements were to be made. We soon became a close-knit group, except for Lady Longdon. Robin seldom visited his mother, nor did I, and only through Mrs. Childs did I learn that the old lady was failing. "Yes, Miss Jennifer," she remarked one day. "I just don't like the looks of her. Lady Longdon is paler and thinner than ever and she picks at her food like a baby, but let me tell you, that old lady hasn't lost her nasty tongue." I decided to go up and see for myself.

I remember knocking on Lady Longdon's door wondering what kind of reception I would receive, and even though she was mean and spiteful, I could not help feeling sorry for her. I stood waiting outside her door, ready to forgive and forget all the unpleasantness between us, when suddenly the door burst open and there she stood, glaring at me like a tiger.

"Well, what do you want? I'm still alive, if that's what's worrying you." I asked her if I could come in and talk to her. "No!" she cried. "You may not come in and talk to me. How dare you come sniveling at my door! You stole John from under my nose and you expect me to be friends with you? Never."

"You're wrong, Lady Longdon," I replied quietly. "I did not propose marriage. John did."

"Ha! Very likely, indeed!" she retorted. "I've met your kind before." Lady Longdon drew herself up haughtily. "I presume you know where John is?" She narrowed her eyes.

"He is away just now," I said lamely.

"Yes, that he is." She shot back. "John is with Lucille Merridith. He has gone to her. You didn't think I knew that, did you?" She drew down her mouth, adding spitefully, "Well, go on son stealer. Go and fight over him and see if your dubious charms will bring him back home again." I turned and fled down the stairs with Lady Longdon's words ringing in my ears. "I hope you fall and break your neck like Adelaide did!" Then her door banged shut.

Later that day, I received an official-looking letter in the post about John. Bringing it in the drawing-room, I closed the sliding doors and opened the envelope.

Dear Mrs. Longdon,

I regret to inform you that your husband, John W. London, expired in his sleep on November 10th, 1866, at Hadley Hospital, London. Funeral arrangements were carried out in accordance with his wishes. He is interred in Greenbough cemetery, North Chapel, Sussex, England.

If I can be of further help, please write to me.

Respectfully yours,

Robert M. Sterling,

Hadley Hospital, London

I dropped down in a chair, completely stunned. John dead? It was unthinkable. I began to cry, not for myself, but for little John. Leaning my elbow on the arm of the chair, I put my head in my hand, pondering our future. Just then, Robin limped into the drawing-room and saw me. "What is wrong, Jennifer?" he asked anxiously. I gazed up at him and handed him the letter. He took it, read it, and dropped it on the floor, speechless with shock. I had never seen a man shed tears before. It was a painful sight. After a while, Robin suggested we go and tell uncle Thorne. We went slowly up the stairs and knocked on his door. The old man squinted at us as we entered his room. His smile faded away, and he asked, "What is it, Robin?"

"John is dead. Jennifer received the news about an hour ago," said Robin flatly.

Uncle Thorne dropped down in his chair, shaking his head from side to side. "Oh John, you poor fool," he mumbled under his breath. Then he took hold of my hand and said, "John needed you, Jennifer. Not that other woman. But he was just too stubborn to see it. It is a mistake for a man to waste his life on a dream and lose his common sense." I gazed down at uncle Thorne and saw how agitated he was. I asked him if he would like some hot tea? He refused, saying he would be all right.

Letting go of my hand, he tugged at Robin's sleeve and asked, "Have you told your mother yet?"

Robin hesitated and then replied. "No. I will tell her tomorrow. It can wait until then."

"Oh no, it can not," said the old man. "She must be told immediately. I'll do it myself. Now, please go. I want to think." Robin and I crept silently out of the room.

Later that night in my bedroom, I looked into my mirror, asking myself a lot of questions. Since I could not answer them, I resolved to push John's death into the back of my mind and start all over again. Slipping into my nightclothes, I brushed my thick red hair and twisted it into a braid. I went to say goodnight to little John. I entered his room and saw him sitting in the middle of his bed poring over a new reader his tutor had given him. I sat down on the bed and gently took the book away from him. "Little John," I began softly. "I have something very important to tell you." The words were coming much easier than I thought. Little John stared at me, alarmed. "What is it, mommy?" he asked in his high squeaky voice. "Is Mr. Price going to go away from here?"

Laying my head on his curly head, I smiled. "No dear. Mr. Price is not going to leave us. He will be your teacher for a long time."

"Oh, goody!" shouted little John, bouncing up and down on the mattress like cricket. "Mr. Price is so much fun. He plays ball with me and all sorts of things and..."

I cut him off gently. "Yes, dear, I know all about it. We are very lucky to have Mr. Price here."

Little John peered in my face. "What's the matter mommy? Have you got a tummy ache?" I pulled him to me, held him close and explained that his father had died and that as long as he lived, he should love him and treasure his memory. After a moment of silence, little John wriggled out of my arms and got down on his knees beside the bed, "Please dear God," he started praying, "If you happen to meet my daddy up there, will you tell him all about me? Thank you. Amen." I bit my lip so hard it almost bled. Was it possible little John really missed his father when they were so seldom together? Tucking him in bed, I leaned down and kissed the face that was so much like John's, then I turned out the light and returned to my room. I sat down in the shadow of the green-glass lamp. It cast an eerie light on John's bookcase over by the door. I could hardly discern the costly leather-bound volumes inside of it. On impulse, I went over and selected a book at random. As I opened it, a small yellowed piece of paper floated to the floor. I picked it up and read:

To Lucille,

You fill my heart with the sweetness of summer,

And the touch of your soft red lips on mine,

Delights my very soul;

Making time stand still.

-John

Well, the irony of it. I thought, as I placed the slip of paper back into the book, which incidentally, was titled *Marriage Vows or Until death do us part* and slid it back in place. I turned out the green-glass lamp and went to bed awaiting tomorrow.

⁂

The months rolled by uneventfully. I kept busy, and somehow or another was placidly happy. Robin and Marie and I became inseparable. We spent many hours together in the drawing-room on cold winter evenings reading aloud to each other, or sometimes playing cards. In the summer, we often drove to Sussex on shopping sprees. Marie and I eagerly explored the shops while patiently Robin sat waiting for us in the carriage.

On these occasions, I would leave little John at home with Mr. Price, which I'm sure made them very happy. Mr. Price doted on my son and vice versa. Now sixteen years old, lovely Marie had grown tall and slender, with a mass of golden wavy hair cascading down her back to her waist. Her delicate pale skin and patrician features, so like her grandmothers' in her youth, caused heads to turn when we went shopping. Yet Marie was not conceited. She accepted her vivid appeal in the same way she accepted life. Since outgrowing the awkward stage, Marie's personality had smoothed out. An avid reader, she spent a lot of time in the library devouring the classics and whatever scientific works she could lay her hands on, and with the help of Mr. Price (whom I noticed took more than a casual interest in her) her world expanded. I would often watch their two heads pouring over a textbook and thought how they fused together like the rich colors on canvas. But aside from that, I realized something new was happening to me, for every time I glanced in Robin's direction, something snapped inside of me. It was as if I had never known John. All I could see was Robin standing alone, needing me and I needing him and so did little John. We needed Robin's love. It was as simple as that.

On a velvety June evening in the summer of 1867, I went for a walk in the cool woods. I felt jumpy and exhausted. I dropped down on the first tree stump I came to; I wanted to be alone for a while. The place was alive with chattering birds. They called out to each other in high-pitched tones and the raucous crows joined in. Folding my hands in my lap, I sat very still and listened to the feathery furor going on around me. Leaning back, I gazed

up at the dense green overhead and spotted a dusky little creature perched on a twig. His tiny breast swelled with pride and
love; and I too was swelled with love for Robin. He and I had
become very close friends in the last year. I leaned on him and I
knew he leaned on me. We were a team. Robin had advised me
earnestly and sensibly as to the household matters, and I soon
learned how to manage a large domain. Whenever we would
meet, whether accidentally or not, his golden eyes would hold
mine in a way that made me tremble.

It began to get dark and a foggy chill settled in the trees, but I
still did not want to move. I smiled, thinking how naïve I was
when I had first climbed the steps of Longdon Hall. I came
there a mere child trusting everybody, but I soon learned, and
grew up painfully fast. Sighing, I moved the dead leaves around
with my foot, enjoying their earthly smell. Dead leaves and dead
dreams go together, I thought. I leaned down and picked up one
and traced its spine with my finger. It was stiff and dry. I
dropped it hurriedly and stood up, then, as I turned to go, I
suddenly became face to face with Robin. He was leaning on his
crutches, staring hard into my face. "Oh, Jennifer," he whispered
brokenly. "Isn't it about time you came home?"

I stumbled across the tiny clearing into his arms. Hot tears
stinging my eyes and if I live to be a hundred, I'll never forget
the look on his handsome face as he pressed his mouth hungrily
on mine. We stood clinging to one another until the night birds
told us to go home.

Robin and I were married about a month later in Sussex and had
a brief honeymoon there. Right from the start, Robin showered
me with loving attention. He insisted on buying me a complete
new wardrobe even though the one I had was presentable. "I
want my little wife to shine like the sun," he remarked as we
entered an exclusive dress salon on the last day of our honeymoon. I protested, but Robin had his way. I remember the stun-

ning green gown he chose for me. I've kept it all these years. It had rows of of narrow green-velvet ribbon sewn on the full-blown skirt and a tight-fitting bodice, which clung to my slim figure like a second skin. It buttoned down the front with tiny velvet buttons and a cream-colored lace collar that fastened at the throat with a diamond brooch. Robin chose the most expensive matching green bonnet he could find to round out the costume. He did not stop there because I arrived home with ten new outfits ranging from subtle shades of brown, yellow, blue, and green to white with all of which flattered my particular coloring.

Marie, her lovely face wreathed in smiles. Greeted us in the foyer when we came home. Throwing her arms around us, she cried, "Oh! You two look so good together. I feel like I'm being born all over again. Daddy, please go and do something. I want to talk to my new mother alone," she said, dragging me toward the drawing-room. Robin laughed and walked away. My eyes followed him out of sight. "Oh, come on, Jennifer," giggled Marie. "You and daddy will have plenty of time to get acquainted." I smiled at her impish look. When we were seated in the drawing-room, the lovely girl took my hand in hers. She began soberly, "Jennifer, I want to thank you for making daddy happy again." She paused, her eyes deep in mine. "Another thing, I accused you of making a play for daddy. Well, I want to apologize for that. I was a nasty little brat, wasn't I Jennifer?"

I had to nod my head because what she said was true. "Marie," I replied. "We all make mistakes growing up. Stop thinking of what your were and concentrate on what you have become. You are a lovely, intelligent girl, and I love you very much." Tears came to her eyes. I had a feeling she was thinking of Adelaide. Then she edged closer to me and buried her face in my neck. "Jennifer," I could barely hear her. "I love you too. All I ask is that you will always keep my daddy happy and smiling. You'll never know how much I cried when he first came home from that awful war with only one leg. I thought I'd never be able to stand it. I knew daddy saw through me, but never once did he mention it. I often felt his eyes upon me. It was so hard to play make believe."

I dabbed her eyes with my handkerchief. "All that is in the past and should be forgotten. From now on, we three will live for today and the devil take tomorrow. You see? I've learned a lot, too."

Marie patted my cheek and grinned. "Yes, Jennifer, the devil take tomorrow." She got up and smoothed her pale-pink hoop dress. Calmer now and looking very pretty, Marie crossed the wide drawing-room and rang for tea.

Robin waited a month to tell his mother of our marriage. He told me she coldly turned her back on him at first, calling him a fool and other names. Then, without warning, she swung around and started pounding his chest, almost knocking him off his crutches. He said she glared at him and screamed at the top of her voice how much she hated him. Robin vowed he would never go near his mother again. He didn't; it was as if she had never lived. I finally realized what love was all about married to Robin. We gave one another stability, companionship, and trust. I had no regrets whatsoever. Moreover, I never had to worry or fret about his not coming home to me when he was absent from Longdon Hall. Though we avoided mentioning Adelaide, it wasn't because we didn't still love her, but that her lonely grave at the side of the house was a constant reminder of Lady Longdon's viciousness. Yet, Robin and I did indeed visit her grave, but stood silently hand in hand beside it, a prayer in our hearts.

Well, as time went on, we lost dear uncle Thorne. He did quietly in his sleep on a cold night in 1869. How I missed him. And right after that, Lady Longdon's mind snapped. A cold shiver still runs up my spine when I think about that awful day I came down the winding stairway, my mind far away, and saw her standing up at the bottom of the stairs, a knife in her hand. She stared up at me savagely and raised her arm to strike out at me. I let out a piercing scream and stumbled backwards on the stairs. Luckily for me, Mrs. Childs suddenly came up behind Lady Longdon and wrestled the knife from her hand. It took all of her strength to do it. Meanwhile, Robin came in the front door right in the middle of the commotion. He lost no time in quelling his frenzied mother.

I fell on the stair and dropped down on my knees, sick with fright. What if Mrs. Childs hadn't appeared in time? I might have been killed. I heard Robin's voice. "Jennifer, are you all right?" he called out. One arm tight around his mother's waist. Mrs. Childs looked up at me. I nodded, not able to speak. Suddenly, Lady Longdon went limp as a wet leaf permitting Robin and Mrs. Childs to lead her slowly up the steps. I got up and leaned hard against the banister as she went past me, her chin on her bony chest. Then, the sight of poor Robin struggling to hold on to his mother and balance himself at the same time woke me up. I told him I would help Mrs. Childs with his mother, even though I hated touching her.

Lady Longdon never left her room again. She passed away two months later, leaving a trail of bitter memories behind her.

Well, that was twenty years ago. It is now 1889 and I am alone. Marie married Mr. Price and went to live in Italy. Little John, now twenty-eight, is a successful architect. He married a girl from Australia and went there to live.

Three years ago, I lost my beloved Robin on that cursed stairway in the rotunda. Whether he became dizzy or tripped on the carpet, I'll never know, but nevertheless, he was dead when I found him at the bottom of the stairs. I went into a severe state of shock afterwards and if it had not been for my two good friends, Mrs. Childs and Mrs. Bevins, I'm sure I would have died, too. They say time heals. Perhaps it does, a little.

I'm sitting writing this in the old drawing-room. My chair is close to the open window, it's such a lovely day. The elm trees lining the drive are dressed in vivid green again and the air is filled with the scent of June roses. Summer, with all of her charm and magic, is bowing to us.

Well, I see it's nearly four o'clock. Mrs. Childs will soon bring in our afternoon tea and afterwards, we'll play a game of cards.

ABOUT THE AUTHOR

Born Madeline Grace McCann in Toronto, Ontario Canada. She was orphaned at the age of ten, she was raised by her maternal grandmother. At the age of 21 she left Canada for the United States and settled in Chicago, Illinois. There she met her future husband James Vincent Anians. Madeline had one son and six grandchildren. She worked for Illinois Bell until she retired in 1967. Her husband James passed away in 1969. Madeline pursued her lifelong hobbies to write stories. She worked at Quality Discount in Chicago in the late 1970s and moved to South Carolina to be close to her family in the 1990s. Madeline passed away in Seneca, South Carolina in the spring of 1999.